Unknown Enemy

A Green Dory Inn Mystery: Book 1

Janet Sketchley
janetsketchley.ca

Unknown Enemy, A Green Dory Inn Mystery

ISBN (epub) 978-0-9951970-6-0
ISBN (mobi) 978-0-9951970-7-7
ISBN (print) 978-0-9951970-5-3

The characters and situations in this book are works of fiction and are not intended to represent any individuals, living or dead. The opinions expressed by the characters are not necessarily those of the author, nor is the grammar they use always correct. The Green Dory Inn and most other places mentioned in this novel are purely fictional and in no way intended to represent real locations. Where real locations are mentioned, they are used fictitiously for the purposes of the story. Some liberty has been taken with the geography around the inn.

Edited by Marcy Kennedy.

Cover by E.A. Hendryx Creative.
Interior dory image: iStock.com/Gunay Aliyeva.
Author photo by Amanda Walker Photography.

Published in Canada by Janet Sketchley.

FICTION/CHRISTIAN/SUSPENSE

Janet Sketchley

janetsketchley.ca

Books by Janet Sketchley

The Redemption's Edge Series:

Heaven's Prey
Secrets and Lies
Without Proof

The Green Dory Inn Mystery Series:

Unknown Enemy
Hidden Secrets
Bitter Truth
Book 4

Non-fiction:

A Year of Tenacity: 365 Daily Devotions

Tenacity at Christmas: 31 Daily Devotions for December

Reads to Remember:
A book lover's journal to track your next 100 reads
(Available in two cover options, print only)

Note to Readers

Lunenburg, Nova Scotia, is a real town—a UNESCO World Heritage site. The Green Dory Inn and most other places mentioned in this novel are purely fictional and in no way intended to represent real locations.

I have taken some liberty with the geography around the inn, for reasons that will become clear by the end of the next book. Speaking of the next book, it's worth noting that while *Unknown Enemy* is a short read to introduce the series, the rest of the series will be full novels.

Also, for my non-Canadian readers, please note I'm using Canadian spellings in this book. You'll see words like colour, neighbour, licence, and travelling, and they're not typos. You'll also see some hyphenated words like mid-fifties and mid-size. That said, and despite the many eyes that have checked the manuscript, I can't guarantee perfection. But I've done my best!

Chapter 1

Thursday

DRY-MOUTHED, LANDON watched the runway speed beneath her window. Vibration from the landing gear drilled into her core.

She shouldn't have come back. But she couldn't refuse, not when Anna needed her.

The plane's intercom crackled. "This is your captain speaking. Welcome to Halifax. Local time is two twelve."

Around her, seat belts clicked open despite the warning lights. A few people stood and rummaged in the overhead bins. The plane hadn't fully stopped. What was the hurry?

Yet the other passengers' sense of urgency had her reaching for her purse.

She followed the herd into the terminal, pulling her borrowed carry-on and checking the overhead signs. When she reached the baggage area, she stood against the wall, watching reunions. Friends, lovers. Two women, clearly mother and daughter, crying as they embraced. She turned away.

A scruffy-haired man with glasses hurried toward the meeting point. He dodged a woman with a pet carrier and stopped beside a pillar. Scanning the crowd, he raised a white cardboard sign: *Landon Smith.*

Anna's neighbour had promised to send his grandson to meet her at the airport. Funny, she'd expected a teenager. This guy was closer to thirty, five or six years older than she was. Tousled hair and a few days' growth of beard made him look like he'd just crawled out of bed.

He gave the room another once-over, and then angled himself to face the passengers still straggling through the arrival gates.

She grasped the handle of her carry-on and walked up beside him. "Hi. I'm Landon."

He turned to her and froze, wide-eyed, a half-formed smile suddenly dead on his lips.

Really? Landon had been gone almost ten years, but this guy had clearly heard something about her. Truth or speculation, he must have thought he could handle it until they were face to face.

It could be a long, silent drive to Anna's inn.

Landon glanced around at the crowd, giving him time to compose himself. When she looked back, his cheeks had darkened to an ugly, mottled red.

Stepping back, he swallowed hard, not meeting her eyes. "Roy asked me to meet you." He lowered the sign as if he'd just realized his arm was still in the air. "Bobby. Bobby Hawke."

He waved a hand toward the luggage carousels. "What colour's your bag?"

Landon danced the little black carry-on on its wheels. "I have everything here."

Bobby looked at the luggage, eyebrows raised.

She flipped her hair with her free hand and forced a bright tone. "I'm only here for a few days. Why bring all my worldly goods?"

"My girlfriend needs a full-sized case for one night, and my mother's just as bad." He turned toward the door. "Let's go, then."

He set a brisk pace from arrivals to the parking garage.

They weren't outside long, but the misty air raised goosebumps on Landon's bare arms. "It was hot and sunny in Toronto."

He paid at the ticket station and she followed him along the rows of cars. Ahead of them, a white Corvette beeped and flashed its lights.

The trunk lid opened, and Landon gave her carry-on a push that sent it skittering to Bobby's side.

He stowed it and headed for the driver's door. "Hop in."

The guy hadn't made eye contact since he broke out of his initial stare. She'd had awkward encounters before, but the emotion bleeding through his barriers felt like fear. Or shame. It stirred her homecoming dread into queasiness.

She buckled her seat belt as loosely as she could and gripped her purse on her lap.

They'd been on the highway for a good fifteen minutes before he opened his mouth. "How was your flight?"

"Fine." She hadn't flown before, but he didn't need to know that. "Thank you for picking me up. This is most of your day."

He pulled out to pass an SUV, driving fast, but without the typical sports car swagger. "It's only a few hours, and I like a good highway run."

Landon tried to block out their destination and concentrate on the ride. Her seat felt like it'd be amazingly comfortable if she could relax.

When she couldn't take any more silence, she cleared her throat. "Whatever you heard about me..."

Bobby's fingers whitened on the wheel. "It's not you."

His tone slammed the door between them.

She shut her mouth and stared at the trees streaking past.

Eventually Bobby let out a soft groan. "I'm sorry. You look like someone I used to know." His laugh sounded forced. "I guess you have an evil twin."

A strangled gasp became a giggle that she barely caught in time. She turned it into a cough.

He'd never understand her crazy relief, and it'd sound like she was minimizing his pain. Plus, it could get him asking questions she didn't want to answer. Still, she had to say something. "I get it. The past has long fingers."

She sneaked a glance at him. The set of his stubbled jaw and the pinch at the corner of his mouth said his wound ran deep.

He wouldn't want her sympathy, nor words of comfort from a stranger.

At least the silence had lost its threatening undertone. Landon turned her gaze out the window again. The mixed forests, the occasional glimpses of water along the way, even the names of towns they passed, whispered "home." Her breathing quickened. This would never be home again.

Lunenburg held nothing for her but pain and memories of lost innocence. The worst had come later, but this was the flash point. Because of that, Landon had vowed to never return.

Until Anna's need overrode her fear.

At least Anna's inn was a neutral place unconnected to the past. Anna and her husband hadn't lived there when Landon was a child.

Bobby avoided the town of Lunenburg and drove along a winding coastal road. By the time he slowed at the Green Dory Inn sign, she was practically vibrating in her seat.

As long as Landon could remember, Anna had been a family friend. She'd taken the girls to vacation Bible school, sometimes to church when their parents agreed, although her own children were a few years older.

When Landon's world shattered, it was Anna who became her surrogate mother, mentor, and confidante. Always ready to listen, or talk, or pray—once Landon was open to prayer.

Anna's prayers were a big part of the reason Landon was whole today. And now something had Anna's neighbour worried enough to beg Landon to come.

"What's going on with Anna, Bobby? Roy didn't want to

skew my perceptions, but it means I'm going in blind."

"He thinks it's emotional more than physical. I've only been here a few weeks, but yeah, maybe. Or maybe she just needs cheering up. Seeing you could turn it around."

Emotional? Anna was one of the most cheerful, stable people Landon knew. Still, sudden widowhood would rock anyone's world.

The long, narrow driveway led past a green fishing dory, brimming with yellow and orange flowers in the middle of the lawn. Beyond it rose a grey-sided house, two storeys with twin dormer windows framing the traditional "Lunenburg bump" extended dormer above a sunshine-yellow front door.

Instead of parking with the other car in the lot behind the house, Bobby stopped beside the walkway to the front door. "Leave your suitcase for now. Let's see if we can get in before she knows it's you."

Landon heard the little boy in him, bursting to surprise a favourite teacher with a gift. It made a nice change from Mr. Prickly. "She knows someone's coming?"

"Gramp didn't want to spring an unexpected guest on her. She thinks I'm bringing my girlfriend."

They hurried along the walkway and up the wide, shallow front steps. A chime sounded as they stepped into a spacious hallway.

From the rear of the house, a voice called, "Hello."

Anna bustled toward them, sandals slapping on the hardwood floor. A black cat with white bib and paws trotted to keep up. "Welcome. How was your—"

She gave a little cry and pulled Landon into a hug. "You're home!"

Landon leaned in, absorbing the unconditional love.

When she stepped back, their gazes held. Anna's eyes were shadowed, and a surprising amount of grey streaked her bobbed brown hair, but her wide, face-lighting smile hadn't dimmed.

Some of the tension unwound in Landon's stomach. She

breathed a silent prayer of thanks. Anna was a constant. She had to be okay.

Anna pressed the cuff of her light cardigan against her eyes. "I thought you were in the middle of another course."

"I have to be back in class on Monday, but at least we'll have the weekend together. And I didn't need to bring too much work with me."

Some of the joy faded from Anna's face. She spread her hands to the rooms on either side of the entryway. "Well, you're here for now, and I'm so glad. I wish I'd known, I'd have bought something special for supper." A tiny frown creased her broad forehead, as if she were mentally inventorying the fridge.

Bobby held out a hand. "You're both invited to eat with Gramp and me tonight, like Jessie would have done if she'd really been your guest. I hope you'll forgive the deceit."

No way would he want to see Landon's face any longer than necessary. She glanced at him. "We can't impose. Especially with Roy's leg in a cast. Kitchen work must be hard."

The clench his jaw beneath the stubble showed how hard it was to meet her eyes, but he did it without changing colour. He even managed a tight smile. "Stew and a fresh loaf from the bread machine. I set everything up before I left. Gramp'll be disappointed if you don't come."

Breakfast had been rushed, and Landon had only brought an apple and some trail mix for her flight. "That sounds great."

Bobby reddened slightly, but it looked like pleasure and not more awkwardness. "A slow cooker is a writer's best friend. Next to a laptop, of course."

Landon felt some heat in her own cheeks. All the silence in the car, and she hadn't even asked what he did. "What do you write?"

His gaze cut to the side. "Science fiction. You probably haven't heard of my books."

"I'm not much of a reader." Oops, that sounded like a put-down. "I go for podcasts and audio books."

"Those are great ways to get the content."

Bobby backed toward the door. "I'll set your suitcase just inside, here, and go tell Gramp we're back. You two can start catching up."

"Thank you, Bobby. We'll see you in about an hour and a half?" Anna's tone held an unfamiliar stiffness.

Landon glanced at her. As soon as they were alone, she asked, "Don't you want to go? Save us cooking?"

"Let me show you around."

Anna led her to the left, into a cozy common room with upholstered chairs and a heavy wooden bookcase. By the window stood a polished oak table with a half-completed jigsaw puzzle of a schooner. Chunks of blue sky and water lay waiting to be filled in.

The main door opened and shut. A minute later, Bobby's car drove back toward the road. The look Anna sent after it wasn't altogether friendly.

Anna, who loved everybody. Landon touched her shoulder. "Is something wrong?"

"Roy should mind his own business." She marched across the hall.

Landon bit her lip. *Emotional*, Bobby had said.

She followed Anna into a cheery breakfast room with white-painted tables and chairs. Each of the pale yellow tablecloths held a little vase of bright blue pansies.

Anna's fingers curled around one of the chair backs. "This was Roy's idea, wasn't it? How did he get in touch with you—dig through my files for your number?"

This suspicious tone was so not Anna. And from everything she'd said about Roy since she and her husband had moved here, the older man was a good friend as well as a good neighbour.

Landon made eye contact, trying to project calm. "He phoned your daughter, but she couldn't get away. She had my phone number from the funeral, so she put us in touch."

"The old gossip! No wonder my kids are fretting at me. Grief takes time. They should know that."

"Anna..." Landon adjusted a vase on one of the tables. "Nobody's conspiring against you. Roy wants to help. That's what friends do. It's what *you* do."

"Did he tell you I'm going crazy? Seeing things at night?"

"No." Her fingers twitched and she caught the vase just before it tipped. Turning to face Anna, she tried for a casual tone. "What have you seen?"

"Lights. Movement in the shadows. Sounds, sometimes. Voices. Whistling. Not every night, but just when I start convincing myself it was my imagination, it happens again."

"You've phoned the police?"

"An officer's been out a few times. He can't find any sign of trespassers. Bobby hasn't found anything either." Her lips twisted. "The only one who believes me is Nigel Foley, and he thinks it's aliens."

Chill settled in Landon's stomach. "You're not on any kind of medication, are you? To help with the grief, or for sleeping?"

Anna's eyes narrowed. "No."

"Hey, it's a fair question."

She waited until Anna gave a reluctant nod. "So if anything happens while I'm here, wake me. You'll have a witness." There must be a rational explanation.

"The guests haven't seen anything, but they're usually in the front rooms with the water view. What I've seen has been in the back."

Anna started toward an arched doorway with white swinging doors. "This inn was Murdoch's dream. It's hard without him, but I'm coping. I've hired a friend's daughter to help when I need her."

Likely another girl who needed someone to believe in her.

Landon followed Anna into a gleaming white and stainless steel kitchen. A wide window over the double sink overlooked a wooden deck, then a grassy stretch leading to an airy, mixed forest. The small parking lot was to the left, with a windowless grey barn at its edge. Along the tree line to the right lay a flower garden and a small shed.

The outbuildings would give easy shelter to anyone skulking around. If he approached through the trees, guests facing the water would never see him.

She turned back to Anna. "The inn and grounds are lovely. Are you busy?"

"It's early in the season. Bookings are slow, but we have enough for now. Meaghan's still learning the ropes, and I'm feeling my age."

Anna was what, fifty-two? She'd never been bouncy, but her steady, purposeful bustle should keep her motoring well into her nineties.

Anna's shoulders straightened, and she seemed to shake off her melancholy. She pulled a key from her pocket. "Let me show you your room. We'll grab your things on the way."

At the top of the stairs lay a wide, open space bordered by four doors, each one ajar to reveal a glimpse of an inviting bedroom. The dormer windows over the main entrance sheltered a cozy conversation nook.

Anna led her to one of the rooms looking out on the forest.

Good. She'd be able to keep an eye out for the prowler.

The bedroom walls were a warm peach, with stretched-canvas prints of brilliant-coloured butterflies. A plain sage duvet on the four-poster bed held a butterfly-shaped pillow, wings outspread. Above the window, the wall sloped inward to the ceiling.

She spun in a slow circle, taking it all in. "It's perfect!"

A smile lit Anna's face. "I'll leave you to settle in. Come down when you're ready."

Alone, Landon ran a hand down a satin-smooth bedpost the colour of aged honey. This room could have been designed for her. A shiver chased across her shoulders.

The glow in Anna's expression at her reaction to the

room. Before that, the tear-filled welcome "home" when she hadn't known Landon was coming. The poorly-veiled disappointment that it was only for the weekend.

She leaned her forehead against the post. Anna was big on reconciliation. Restoration. The woman's prayers had played a huge part in Landon's salvation and healing, as had her wise counsel these past few years. How long had she secretly been praying for Landon to "come home"?

Pain closed her throat. This visit was supposed to help. Not add to Anna's hurt.

~~~

When she couldn't stall any longer, Landon slid her phone into her back pocket, picked up her room key, and headed out. No need to lock the door with no other guests here, but if she set the pattern now, she wouldn't forget later.

The scent of baking wafted up the stairs, and before she reached the kitchen, a timer beeped. When she walked into the room, Anna was taking a pan from the oven.

Landon waited until she'd set it on a trivet before speaking. "Mmm, smells good. What is it?"

"Cinnamon coffee cake. I didn't have time to make anything complicated."

Anna plopped stained blue oven mitts onto the counter and swiped the back of her hand across her forehead. "All settled in?"

Hospitality filled her tone, but there might have been an underlying wistfulness, too. Landon pretended not to notice. "It's a beautiful room. A beautiful inn, Anna. Your guests must love it."

"So far, so good. Would you set the deadbolt on the front door? We'll go out the back way."

When Landon returned, Anna plunged her hands back into the oven mitts and cradled the freshly foil-covered pan. "Let's go."

Apparently Roy was forgiven. Smiling, Landon pulled the
~~~

door open.

Anna stepped through and pitched forward with a cry. She landed hard on her knees. The pan shot from her hands and skidded across the deck.

Landon helped her stand. "What happened? Are you hurt?"

Anna brushed off her knees and turned back to the door. "I tripped—what are they doing here?"

She picked up a red rubber gardening clog, the sole caked in dirt, then reached for its mate. Frowning, she propped them against the deck railing and retrieved the cake pan from where it lay.

"Still right side up, at least." She peeked under the foil. "No harm done. But I know I cleaned the mud off my clogs and set them aside to dry."

She fixed Landon with a look that dared her to argue. "I always do."

"Could Timkin have been playing with them?"

"That cat can be trouble, but even if he'd left them in the way, he wouldn't have muddied them again."

Landon locked the door and followed her down the steps to the grass. "It's a silly prank for someone to play. You're sure you weren't distracted and forgot? If the phone rang, or you had to go to the bathroom—"

Anna's sigh sounded like the earth itself groaning. "I don't think so, but it's possible."

Landon squeezed her elbow. "It happens to everyone."

"I know. Just don't tell Roy, okay? He's been acting like a mother hen since Murdoch died."

"It'll be our secret."

Anna led the way to the left, past the barn and into the trees. She might resent Roy's perceived meddling in her life, but the neighbouring homes had enough traffic between them to wear a path among the trunks.

Landon walked beside her through the wide-spaced tree trunks, inhaling the tangy mix of pines and salt air. The scent brought memories of simpler days. Summer games of hide and seek. Family picnics, when they'd still been a family.

It hurt.

No, she couldn't stay, but she could take this visit as a chance to give back to the woman who'd given her so much. They'd enjoy their time together until Sunday, and hopefully they'd both see this prowler. A witness would help Anna's credibility, plus she might be able to spot something that would help the police figure this out.

Anna said it always happened at night, but it didn't make sense that the prowler left no traces. There should at least be a footprint, or flattened grass or something. No wonder nobody else believed her.

Landon scowled at the dirt path. Whoever was playing these tricks on Anna could have set up her shoes this afternoon, too.

As for the lack of witnesses, who else would see? A thin forest bordered the inn on both sides and to the rear, and on the other side of the road the guardrailed shoulder ended in a steep drop to the ocean. When there were no guests, it was an isolated spot for a woman alone.

Too bad Anna didn't have someone living with her long-term to keep her company, but however wishful her thinking, she wouldn't really expect Landon to leave school and move back here.

The trees opened to a ranch-style home with a roofed-in front porch facing the ocean. The houses Bobby had driven past on the way to the inn were all older two-storeys. "Why's this one so different?"

"Roy's place? The old home burned down years ago, and he said he wanted something more practical to get old in. Everything's on the one level, and he only uses the basement for storage. After I've been up and down the stairs to the guest rooms a few times, I start to envy him."

"But your inn has character. There's history in those walls."

Half a dozen steps led up to the back door. It would be easy to add an access ramp here, if Roy's mobility ever required it.

Bobby let them in and showed Anna where to set the cake pan. "You didn't need to bring anything, but that smells great."

He'd regained his composure, but Landon tried to stay out of his line of sight.

A white-haired man in a short-sleeved button shirt shuffled toward them with a walker. He looked a good twenty-five years older than Anna. Old enough to fill the unofficial father role Anna said he'd taken on.

The set of his mouth gave him a formidable expression that matched his gruff voice on the phone. Yet he cared enough about Anna to worry about her and to reach out for help. And to pay for Landon's plane ticket when she admitted the need.

He lifted a hand from the walker frame. "You must be Landon. Good to meet you."

She squashed her nervousness and stepped forward. Up close, his sea-blue eyes gleamed as if he were still sixteen. Or perhaps twelve, given the mischief in his sudden smile.

The strength in his handshake surprised her.

"Thank you again for the flight." She dropped her voice so it wouldn't penetrate Anna's conversation with Bobby. "You're right, she's not herself. I hope I can help."

Roy's jaw twitched. "Losing her husband was enough. I'd hate to see anything else go wrong."

~~~

Landon woke gasping for air. She catapulted from the bed into a defensive stance and scanned the dimly-lit room, waiting for reality to overcome memory.

This was Anna's inn. A safe place.

Pacing softly to the door and back, she concentrated on slowing her breathing, anchoring in the present.
~~~

Quiet night sounds came through the partly-open window. Wind stirred the trees, and in the distance a dog barked. The moon gave enough light to see Anna's parked car and the outbuildings. At the edge of the darkened lawn, the trees made a darker mass.

A human shadow flitted from the barn to the trees. Landon's breath hissed.

Outside, all was still, but she knew she'd seen someone.

Had Anna seen him too?

Landon snatched her phone from the bedside table and left the room. A stained-glass sailboat night light in the open area lit her way to the stairs. She hurried down to the main floor.

Navigating by moonlight, she reached Anna's private quarters at the rear of the inn. She crossed the sitting room to the bedroom door and tapped gently. "Anna? It's me. Don't turn on your light... there's someone outside."

Bedclothes rustled, then Anna pulled the door open, blinking. "Where?"

"By the trees."

Anna charged into the kitchen, slowing before she reached the window.

Landon caught up to her. "I don't see him now."

A nudge at Landon's ankles made her bite back a squeal. Timkin the cat butted his head against her again and moved to Anna's feet with a quiet mew. He trotted to the door.

Anna flicked on the outside light. She hesitated, then shot back the deadbolt and cracked the door open just wide enough for the cat to squeeze through before slamming it shut.

Landon stayed where she could watch through the window. Would the signs of activity scare the intruder away?

The cat walked to the edge of the deck and stood looking into the darkness. Then, tail erect, he jumped between the posts of the railing and streaked for the woods.

"Timkin took off—toward the spot I saw the person moving."

"Then it's someone he knows. He wouldn't run to a stranger." Anna turned the light off. She pulled a giant flashlight from a drawer and grasped the doorknob.

"Anna, don't—"

But she was already on the deck, light lancing toward the trees. "Come out. I know you're there."

Silence. Landon stepped onto the deck beside her, the smooth boards cool against her bare feet. "This is crazy. Of course the cat knows him. He's been bothering you for weeks. Come back inside."

Anna's light swept the tree line. "Where did you see him?"

"A little to the left. There. But—"

"Shh."

Anyone could be out there in the dark, sneaking up on them from another direction. Landon took an involuntary step back toward the safety of the inn. "Anna, please."

"If you come out now, I don't have to call the police. Just come talk to me."

Landon gripped her cell. "But I have a phone right here. Don't make me use it." The guy—or girl—was likely long gone.

Something rasped against a tree trunk. Anna's flashlight beam darted and pinned a slim figure who trudged toward them, one hand shading his eyes.

She aimed the light at his feet, making a path to the deck. "Corey! What on earth were you doing out there?"

He was only a kid, maybe fourteen. Scruffy hair, dark clothes that let him blend into the night. Timkin paced behind him like a rear guard.

As the boy came up the deck stairs, the fear and defeat in his face pulled at Landon's heart.

Shoulders slumped, he spoke to the floorboards. "I wanted to spy on your prowler. Find out what he's after."

"You could have been hurt. Or arrested."

His chin came up. Defiance twisted his mouth, but then his expression drooped. "I could have run."

"Corey, Murdoch would be proud of you for looking out for me, but he wouldn't want you putting yourself at risk like that. Please promise me you won't do it again."

When the boy nodded, Anna thanked him. "This prowler upsets me, but I'd be more upset if anything happened to you. Come inside for hot chocolate."

Corey's gaze met Landon's for a millisecond. He bent to rub the cat's back. "I should go."

They watched him trudge back into the woods, then Landon followed Anna into the kitchen. "And you said nobody believed you."

"They don't say it, but I hear the doubt in their voices. Corey's so loyal to Murdoch, he'd believe me even if I'd imagined the whole thing." Anna's heavy tone said it was no comfort.

"You're sure he hasn't been the prowler all along?"

"Positive. Plus, if he were, he wouldn't have hidden out in the woods to keep watch."

"Some people might. And then take credit for scaring the guy off."

Anna shook her head. "He's just a kid who needs a break."

"I hope so. But your gift is to see the best in people. What they can be, not necessarily what they are."

Anna filled the kettle. "Since we're up, how about some herbal tea? Or can you go straight back to sleep?"

Wisps of nightmare fluttered, and Landon shivered. "A drink would be nice, if you're having one. Or I could just keep watch for a bit and see if the real troublemaker shows."

"We'll turn out the lights and watch together."

Anna pulled a green cardboard box from a drawer and dropped two tea bags into the pot. "Spearmint blend. It's soothing."

Once they carried steaming mugs into the private sitting room, Anna turned out the lights and angled the vertical blinds so they could look out.

"There's no telling when—or if—he'll show up. He's left me alone the past few nights, but I'm so on edge I kept waking anyway."

Landon embraced the quiet, waiting for her eyes to adjust to the dim glow from the clock on the DVD player.

Anna sat beside her on the couch. Timkin jumped onto Anna's lap, turned three tight circles, and lay in a tidy knot. She stroked the black and white fur. "Did Corey wake you? I didn't hear a thing."

Landon set her mug on the coffee table and drew her knees up to her chest. "I was already awake."

"Ah. I wondered if being here would bring more shadows to light. You're strong enough to face them, now."

The back of her neck prickled, and she pressed her fingers against the spot.

After all the counselling, all the prayer and heartache, she'd worked through most of the pain. In her mind, she'd revisited it all, picturing Jesus at her side, letting His healing presence wrap her like a soft blanket still warm from the dryer. His own blood covered her stains, washed her wounds. He called her whole. Precious. His delight.

Remembering the dream, she felt again the sweat-slicked film of fear that would vacuum-seal her into oblivion. "That was too real for a shadow. Anna, I can't go back there, I'd—"

Anna squeezed her hand. "Healing, growth, it's always in layers. You are healed, you're being healed..."

"...and I will be healed." She nodded in time to the words. How many times had she heard that mantra? "But it has to end. I was doing fine. I had a life and a future."

Shivers took her. She picked up her mug and gulped some tea. It hurt to swallow.

This was why she hadn't come for Murdoch's funeral. Anna had enough family support, and she'd accepted Landon's desire to stay away from here. This time there was no one else. Anna's children didn't live nearby, and neither could take time off again so soon.

She couldn't regret coming for Anna, but she couldn't face the pain, either. She clutched Anna's fingers. "Pray for me? We can keep our eyes open in case anything happens outside."

"God will look after the mystery man. Right now we need Him to look after you." Anna bowed her head and lifted her free palm, open to receive. Her words came out calm and sure, naming the need and thanking God for His good response.

As Anna's prayer moved into praise, Landon's peace returned. Warmth wrapped her, and her spirit caught tender words she couldn't quite discern. She leaned back in her seat. "Thank you."

"Dear one, I appreciate you coming more than I can say. I hope you can back up my story about this prowler, but even if he hides until you're gone, I believe this is for your healing. You had a barrier against returning, and now God can work there too."

No point saying it was a reasonable boundary, one she hadn't intended to push. Landon sat up and rubbed her eyes, and glanced out into the darkness. "Maybe your prowler took another night off. About ready to go back to bed?"

"I think so." Anna stood, cradling the sleeping cat, and settled him onto the couch. "Something to pray about, long-term... see what God does here these next few days, and then ask what He thinks about coming back once your courses are done? Lunenburg needs social workers too, and you understand how the rural dynamic affects our youth."

Only Anna would pray her into peace and then press on the heart of the bruise. The request should have undone her, but the warm blanket sensation held her fast. Beneath it, her heart constricted.

She faced Anna and shook her head. "This is not my place. I'm sorry."

Chapter 2

Friday

LANDON WOKE LATE the next morning, head thick from the broken sleep. It didn't help that her body thought it was an hour earlier than the local time zone. Or that she still wore the guilt of disappointing Anna. But she didn't belong here. Last night proved that, and Anna shouldn't have asked.

A quick shower helped her adjust, and she hurried downstairs. In the kitchen, Anna was talking with a plump woman in her early twenties. The younger woman's curly, red hair was already escaping from its simple braid.

Anna broke off at her approach. "Landon, meet Meaghan. We have a reservation tonight, so we have some things to do this morning. I'll get you some breakfast, and then you just relax."

Landon spread her hands. "All I need is tea and toast, and then put me to work."

Something flickered in Meaghan's eyes. Did she think Landon wanted her job?

Landon smiled. "I'm only here for the weekend. Might as well be useful."

Meaghan seemed to relax, but now Landon had rubbed salt into Anna's disappointment.

This wasn't the troubled teen she'd imagined as Anna's friend's daughter, but the slope of Meaghan's shoulders, and the tautness around her wide eyes, revealed her need.

Landon walked to the window just as a figure ambled from the woods, some kind of rod slung over his shoulder. "Who's that?"

"Nigel Foley, and he'll want to talk. It would be a big help if you could keep him company while Meaghan and I get to work. He's a little... lost, sometimes."

This must be the guy who thought Anna's prowler was an alien. "Of course. Why is he wandering in the woods?"

Meaghan snorted. "Oh, he'll tell you. In detail."

Anna called out the back door. "Good morning, Nigel. Come in for tea."

A minute later, footsteps clomped across the deck. The man stomped each boot twice, then stepped out of them and into the kitchen. He set the contraption he'd been carrying inside the door.

Tufts of black hair stuck out under his camouflage-coloured ball cap, and rumpled clothes hung loose on his wiry frame. Sharp grey eyes scanned the room and fixed on Landon.

Anna rested a hand on his arm. "I want you to meet my friend Landon. She's visiting for the weekend. Meaghan and I have work to do, so why don't you two get acquainted?"

Landon put on her brightest smile. "You like tea?"

He tipped his head to the side and stared at her like a robin listening for a worm. She was about to repeat the question when he straightened, blinked three times, and nodded twice. "Anna keeps a special blend for me."

Anna pulled a glass jar half-full of tea leaves from the cupboard and handed it to him. "Meaghan's gone to start cleaning, and I need to bake some cookies. I'll make your tea, and you two can chat in the breakfast room."

Nigel opened the jar, sniffed the contents and gave them a suspicious stare before handing it back to Anna. "Good."

She filled the kettle and set out two small ceramic teapots. "Landon, English Breakfast?"

"Yes, please." She opened the square plastic food keeper Anna had slid toward her and found golden blueberry muffins. "Mr. Foley, would you like some muffins?"

"Anna's cooking?" At Anna's nod, he blinked again. "Safe, then. I'll have two."

Before he'd sit at the table where Landon placed their things, Nigel picked up the little vase of pansies and checked the underside. Then he peered in among the stems. Again the blinks and nods.

He pulled his chair sideways so his back wasn't to the window, and sat. "Can't be too careful." Leaning forward, he peered into her eyes. "How do you know Anna?"

Landon concentrated on pouring her tea. "She's a friend of my mom. She's always been kind to me."

"One of the good ones. Why do you have a man's name?"

Apparently keeping him company meant an interview. Okay, she'd trade question for question. "It was my mother's idea. What was that device you were carrying?"

He glanced out the window, then jammed his hat more firmly onto his head. "Metal detector. They're after something, whoever's troubling Anna. I want to find it first." He picked up a muffin and took a huge bite.

Even with milk, Landon's tea was too hot to do more than sip, but Nigel ate his second muffin and downed his tea without a wince. "Time to go. Mother will be worried."

Landon piled their dishes onto the tray and followed him back to the kitchen.

With a formal farewell to Anna, who was dropping cookie dough onto a baking sheet, Nigel hoisted his metal detector and made his exit.

Landon loaded their plates and Nigel's cup into the dishwasher. "I forgot to ask about his private tea stash."

"Oh, he dries and blends his own ingredients. It's supposed to help the immune system and boost brain power."

Anna slid the cookies into the oven and set the timer. "Thank you for that. Nigel's a lonely man, and I always try to take time for him."

Another misfit for Anna's caring heart. To discover who was skulking around her property at night, maybe they should look for someone who wasn't getting the attention they thought they deserved. Or who was jealous of the time she spent on others.

~~~

Late that afternoon, Landon surfaced from her reading and shut her laptop. Stretching, she left her room and went downstairs. She was here to help Anna, but the course work still had to be done.

She found Anna in the guests' common room, bent over the jigsaw puzzle.

Outside, a motor growled. Landon glimpsed a ride-on mower cut a swath beside the driveway. "Who does your lawn?"

"Corey. It'll be easier for him once summer break starts."

Corey of the late-night reconnaissance. "He's a brave kid, to try keeping watch for you."

"Typical teenager, thinks he's indestructible."

Anna slid her index finger through the loose puzzle pieces. "He's one slip away from juvenile detention. He ran with a bad crowd, but he and Murdoch had a rapport."

Her sigh sounded like it came from the depths of her soul. "I'm carrying on where my husband can't. Now Cory seems to feel it's his legacy to look out for me."

"Maybe that'll help keep him out of trouble."

"That's my prayer. I'll try to find extra work for him around here over the summer." Anna fitted a bit of blue into the puzzle sky.

Shouts from outside pulled them both to the window. The mower stood silent. Nearby, a boy in a red ball cap advanced
~~~

on a smaller figure in a dark hoodie, who bunched up as if ready to fight.

Anna blazed into the entryway and out the front door, Landon right behind her. They reached the boys just as the stranger slammed his palm into Corey's chest, knocking him backward.

Cursing, Corey backpedalled but kept his feet. He lunged at his opponent, but at Anna's cry he pulled up and turned toward her, face red. "Sorry."

Anna closed the gap to the heavier-set boy. "Quinn, I've told you before. Corey has work to do, and I do not want to see this sort of behaviour."

Quinn smirked. "Close the blinds."

Anna pointed toward the road. "Don't come back until you're prepared to be civil. Your grandmother doesn't need me calling about this again."

His eyes narrowed, and he rocked on the balls of his feet like he wanted to throw a punch. Then he pulled a blister pack of gum from his jeans and popped the final piece into his mouth. He threw his trash at Anna's feet and spun on Corey. "Who needs you, anyway?"

He grabbed the scratched-up mountain bike that had been lying at the edge of the driveway, and launched himself toward the road, helmet dangling from the handlebars.

Corey kicked at the grass. "I know, I shouldn't let him get to me, but—" Growling low in his throat, he peeled off his hoodie and dropped it in the fresh-cut grass.

The scrawny arms sticking out of his too-large tee shirt wouldn't have done much damage to the other boy.

Anna picked up the sweatshirt and shook off the clippings. "I'll leave it on the deck rail for you."

"Thanks." He turned back to the mower.

Landon waited until they were half-way to the inn, with the machine droning in the background, to ask, "Could Quinn be your prowler?"

"I don't think so. He's jealous that Corey has this job, but what would it gain him?"

"Spite can be its own reward."

Anna picked another piece of grass off the hoodie. "The worst part is, they used to be friends, until Corey started trying to clean up his life. I think Quinn feels betrayed."

"If Murdoch was part of Corey's turn-around, Quinn might extend that blame to you. To solve this, we have to look at everyone who has a motive. Plus, it sounds like you two have a history, and he seems like the type to hold a grudge."

"If I came out one morning and my tires were flat, I might suspect him, but this night-time stuff is too subtle."

Landon didn't argue, but her mental list of suspects now had a name on it.

~~~

Anna's guests arrived after supper. The Bicks were a middle-aged couple from Saskatchewan, on their first-ever visit to Nova Scotia. Landon had assumed they'd stay in their room, but after carrying their bags upstairs, they came back to the common room for the coffee and cookies Anna had offered.

Landon helped prepare the tray. Anna added two more cups before picking it up. She winked at Landon. "Most guests like to chat."

Once they were settled with drinks and Anna had described some of the local tourist highlights, Mr. and Mrs. Bick took turns relating the high points of their trip so far. Landon let the words wash over her, absorbing the couple's pleasure in their experiences.

She hadn't given much thought before to the difference between a country inn and a hotel. Anna's Green Dory Inn was like being welcomed into someone's home. No wonder guests loved it.

Later, Landon followed Anna to her private sitting room. "How about if I camp on your couch tonight? If your prowler shows up, we'll be able to talk without disturbing your
~~~

guests."

And Anna's nearness might keep the nightmares away. It was worth a try.

The tension around Anna's eyes and mouth faded into a smile. "It'll be like a sleep over. But I hope he'll give us another night off."

Hours later, Anna's scream jolted Landon awake in the darkened sitting room. Feet tangled in her blanket, she fell off the couch. She kicked free and lunged for Anna's door.

She pushed it open and ran to Anna, silhouetted against the window. "What happened?"

"A face!" Anna's breath came in whistling gasps. "I heard scratching at the window, and when I looked out, he was right there. Staring in at me."

The rain-streaked window was black and empty. "Who?"

"I don't know—he wore one of those rubber masks."

Landon drew Anna away from the window, and the curtains swished back into place. In the sitting room, she settled her on the couch and draped the still-warm blanket around her. After peeking out the window and seeing no one, she turned the table lamp on low.

Anna's face was white and tear-streaked, but her breathing had slowed. "Why did I have to scream like that? What if the guests heard me?"

"I'll go and check. Promise you'll stay here. You are not going out there. Got it?"

"I'll wait."

Landon walked into the kitchen and checked the windows there, then slipped through the house to the foot of the stairs. Silence. She crept upward. If the guests had phoned 9-1-1, Anna would be mortified.

At the top of the stairs she released her breath. No voices, no light under the door. They must not have heard.

She retraced her steps, checking each window this time. Still nothing.

Anna hadn't moved. Timkin had emerged from wherever

he'd hidden and lay curled on her lap. Her hand was pressed into his fur. Splotches of colour had returned to her face. "Did they sleep through it?"

"I think so. And it looks like this guy's gone. Did you call the police?"

"I'll wait until morning, after the Bicks leave for their whale-watching tour. If he left any traces, they'll still be there. Not that he's left any yet."

"Then I'll make you some tea."

By the light of the range hood, Landon set the kettle to boil. Good thing she'd wanted to be near Anna tonight, in case of trouble. If she'd heard the scream, running downstairs to help would have wakened the guests. If she hadn't heard, Anna might have tried to take the fight outside again.

Too bad she couldn't have seen the guy, to prove Anna's claim.

If there'd been anyone to see.

She glanced at the sitting room door, as if Anna could have heard her traitorous thought.

It felt disloyal, but only Anna saw these things, and there was never any evidence. Perhaps her defensive attitude toward her neighbours' concern was a cover for her own secret doubts.

Landon dropped some chamomile teabags into the pot. A prowler was bad enough. Anna losing touch with reality would be much worse.

Roy was right. Anna needed help.

The first step would be finding out what kind of help. Without hurting a kind woman's heart.

A weight in her chest made it hard to draw breath.

Staying here could undo her hard-won progress. Maybe even sabotage her current course. "Oh, Anna..."

Tears blurred her vision, and as she blinked them back, the memory of Nigel Foley's mannerisms mocked her.

Maybe they were all crazy. But no matter the cost, she had

to stay. She couldn't leave Anna without finding out the truth.

Chapter 3

Saturday

In the morning, Anna seized Landon's offer to help with breakfast for the guests. "Not that it needs two of us for one couple, but I'll enjoy your company."

Landon arranged place settings at the table with the best view of the ocean, and refreshed the flowers in the vases. Quiet instrumental music added a gentle ambiance.

Once the couple came downstairs and placed their order, Anna's instructions with the food seemed overly enthusiastic.

Landon kept quiet and filled two small bowls with yogourt and fruit. If the cheery approach was meant to convince her how wonderful it would be to come back here permanently, it wouldn't work.

She set the bowls and two glasses of apple juice on a wooden tray, and returned the containers to the fridge.

Her eyes burned, after only two nights of fractured sleep. Anna must be exhausted. No wonder she was on edge. This morning's too-sunny disposition was probably more about coping than persuasion.

Anna whisked the tray into the breakfast room, and then started cooking. "Have some tea, if you like. I've got this."

"No, I'll wait for you."

Bacon sizzled and popped on the grill. Anna buttered toast, and flipped eggs like a pro. She slid everything onto the warmed and waiting plates, and carried the food in to her guests.

Her light chatter floated into the kitchen where Landon wiped down the countertops.

Whatever was happening after dark, Anna seemed fully grounded during the day. Except for things like the forgotten garden clogs.

It had to be a prowler. Surely there'd be other signs, if she were losing touch with reality.

Anna brought the empty bowls back with her and slid them into the dishwasher. "That'll keep them going for a little while."

She poured herself a cup of tea and sat at the table.

Landon's mouth stuck shut. She hadn't said anything last night about her decision to stay. Once she spoke, there'd be no turning back. She rinsed the dish cloth, wrung it out and draped it over the divider in the double sink.

She braced her hands behind her against the edge of the counter. "I—I can stay a little longer. Help get to the bottom of this."

At first Anna didn't react. Then a trembling smile split her face. Her eyes welled. "It would mean so much not to be alone."

"I'll need to do some laundry. Maybe I shouldn't have packed so light."

"That, my dear, is the least of our worries. But what about your course? How much time could you miss?"

"I'll email my prof. These shorter sessions are pretty intensive, but I can keep up with reading and do my paper. I don't want to leave you here by yourself overnight. Unless Meaghan could move in for a while?"

"I don't think her boyfriend would go for that."

The weary caution in Meaghan's eyes... "He's not abusive, is he?"

Anna's lips tightened. "I think he just likes to be waited on. And he doesn't seem happy about her working here."

"Then I need to stay. Which means I need to talk to Roy. He bought my ticket." And Anna had been uncharacteristically angry with him for getting involved. "There must be a way to change it."

"For a fee. I can cover that for you. But only if your professor agrees. Your course comes first."

"Class will be okay." Landon freed her hair from its ponytail and finger-combed it. Her student loan covered basic living expenses, but airfare and cancellation fees were not in her budget. "I hate not having any money."

Anna bobbed her head gently, as if remembering her kids' university days. "The lament of students everywhere."

By the time the kitchen was cleaned and the guests had gone, Landon was yawning. Anna's call to the police had received a promise of a patrol car sometime in the next hour or so.

Landon headed for her room. "I need to email my professor."

Once she sent the message, she lay down to rest, one ear open for the sound of the promised police car.

The next thing she heard was a tap at her door. "Landon? They're here."

"They" turned out to be a car with one officer. Landon and Anna came out the back door just as he climbed the steps to the deck. Clearly he'd been here enough to discover the more convenient rear entrance.

Tall and serious-looking, with black hair and deep brown eyes, he introduced himself to Landon as Constable Dylan Tremblay.

Anna led the way into the sitting room. She stood behind her chair, gripping the backrest.

The officer listened to her story and jotted a few notes, then turned to Landon with a little smile. "Not how we like to welcome visitors to the area, Ms. Smith."

His gaze lingered on her face. "Did you see anything?"

She'd feel better if he were a seasoned veteran, not someone young enough her peers would want to date. "No. He was gone by the time I reached Anna."

His expression didn't change, but his exhale seemed a bit more forceful than necessary.

As if he didn't believe there'd been someone there to begin with.

Landon pointed to Anna's couch. "I was sleeping here so I wouldn't disturb the guests if there was trouble."

"So you were already concerned."

"Anna told me about the other incidents when I arrived on Thursday. Constable, we broke up a quarrel yesterday. Two boys, Corey and Quinn."

Anna's lips tightened, but what did she expect? They had to give the police any small clues they had.

Constable Tremblay was nodding, as if he knew the boys and what Landon wanted to say.

She said it anyway. "Quinn was rude to Anna. Hostile and spiteful, the sort of attitude that could be behind this."

"We keep in fairly close contact with both boys. I'll talk to them."

He followed Anna to her bedroom window. "May I?" He cranked open the pane and removed the screen to poke his head out. "Nothing I can see from here. He'd have needed a ladder. I'll go—"

Footsteps raced across the deck and the back door banged. "Anna?"

They met Meaghan in the kitchen. When she saw Anna, some of the fear left her face. Hand to her heart, she sank onto one of the chairs. "What happened?"

Anna sat across from her and took her other hand. "Our prowler stuck his face in my window last night."

Meaghan blanched. "Did you recognize him?"

"He wore a mask." Anna turned. "Constable Dylan Tremblay, this is my housekeeper, Meaghan Lohnes."

The officer's notebook was back in his hand. "Ms. Lohnes, can you tell me anything that might help?"

One forefinger twisting a lock of her red hair, she focused on the table. "It only happens at night, when I'm not here. We haven't seen anything during the day."

He made a note. "I'll look around outside."

As Anna followed him out, Meaghan stood. "I'd better get to work."

Landon bit her lip. "Meaghan... do you think there's really someone there? I mean, could Anna be imagining this? Nobody else has seen him."

Meaghan's gaze darted around the kitchen. "She's a good person. This shouldn't be happening."

"But we need to know if it's a physical threat or if it's her health. I can stay a little longer, but—how do we help her?"

"I wish I had an answer."

Meaghan collected her cleaning supplies from the cupboard and hurried from the room.

Landon went outside to hear what the constable had to say.

He rested a foot on the stairs to the deck. "No footprints, no marks from a ladder. The grass isn't mashed down, but he could have scuffed it up afterwards. That's not much help, I know. You ladies keep your doors locked at night."

He levelled a serious look at Anna. "And no trying to engage him if he returns."

Whether he believed Anna or not, he had her pegged. And he cared about her safety.

Once he left, Landon followed the path through the trees to visit Roy. She found him on the long front porch.

Instead of watching the sailboats, Roy was re-potting African violets.

The man had an incredibly square jaw, and smiling squared it further. "Perfect timing. I need another small pot from the basement, and the doctor would have my hide if I tried the stairs on my own. Would you be so kind? Save me using a teacup?"

When she came upstairs, he was in the kitchen pouring two glasses of water. He tapped a fingernail against the nearest glass. "If you'll carry these, I'll take the plant pot."

Landon picked up the drinks and matched his shuffling pace as he pushed his walker back to the porch. "You've lost your helper today."

"He set everything up for me here and went to the gym in town."

Bobby hadn't struck Landon as the gym type, but he'd be relieved to miss her. It had taken obvious effort on his part to be sociable when she and Anna came for supper that night. Full marks for extending the invitation in those circumstances.

She took a chair near Roy's work table. With any luck, she'd be gone before Bobby came back, and spare him the discomfort of seeing her again.

Roy trowelled dirt into the new pot and carefully stuck the severed stem end of a leaf in the middle. "Everything all right at the inn?"

"Well, no. That's why I'm here."

Piercing sea-blue eyes met hers. He nodded, as if waiting for her words.

"Anna saw a face in her window last night. Wearing a mask. He was gone before I saw him. If he was there. There's never any evidence. Could she be imagining it?"

It felt disloyal to voice the possibility.

Roy stared out at the water. "I don't know. You see what I meant, though. She's not herself."

"And I can't tell if that's because of her prowler, or if some other problem is causing her to imagine a prowler. I need to stay longer, until we know what's going on. Could you change my ticket? Anna said if I can't cover the fee, she will."

"I'll cancel it, and they'll give us a partial credit for when we re-book. Unless you decide to stay." He winked.

Landon's stomach flipped. She sipped her water and

stared at the variety of blossoms on the table. Purple, blue, pink. A white one. "She wants me to move back when I finish my degree. But I can't."

"It would be hard. And maybe your place is elsewhere. She won't pressure you."

No, but guilt might. Or God. "Roy, are you a Christian?"

"Gonna convert me if I'm not?"

The gruff question drew her to make eye contact. "I was going to ask you to pray for us if you are."

He winked. "Already on it. Anna and Murdoch and me, we kind of adopted one another when they moved in. She told me some of your story. You're on my list too."

Landon flinched and nearly dropped her water glass.

"Good save. Don't blame Anna for speaking out of turn. One day we were talking about the kids she and Murdoch have worked with and I asked if she'd known the girl who went missing. She got real quiet, but then she set me straight on the rumours I'd heard and shared how well you were doing. She's proud of you, Landon."

He tapped a finger to his lips. "And I won't breathe a word."

Right. Like he'd kept quiet about Anna's situation. Landon gave herself a mental shake. That was different. Anna's family—and Landon, since they couldn't come—had needed to know.

Still, she couldn't look him in the eye. "Thank you. I need to get back now. Meaghan will be ready to go home, and Anna has a headache. We didn't want to leave her alone."

He shuffled to his feet. "I have a phone, you know."

"If I'd phoned, you'd have a baby plant in a teacup."

Besides, she'd needed the breather, needed to ask Roy's honest assessment of Anna without being overheard. Except he didn't know any more than she did. Which meant she'd have to question Anna directly. And keep watch tonight for the prowler.

~~~

A pale blue sedan sat beside Anna's, facing the barn, when Landon returned to the inn. An older model, on the large side, and the way the front end dipped, it looked tired.

Maybe it was the size of the car, but the figure behind the wheel didn't seem big enough to be able to see over the dashboard.

Closer-up, he was a small, dark-haired man about her age, slouched in his seat. One arm rested in the open window frame.

He squinted at her. "Tell Meaghan to hurry it up. I've got places to be." He lifted a cell phone and started tapping the screen.

She clamped her mouth shut and marched toward the inn. This bundle of sweetness must be Meaghan's boyfriend. He might not be abusive, but if he was this rude to strangers, he'd be at least verbally toxic at home.

Crossing the back deck, she exhaled her irritation. Good thing Meaghan had someone supportive like Anna to keep an eye on her wellbeing and speak kindness into her life.

The inn was silent. In case Anna was resting, Landon avoided the sitting room and slipped up the stairs.

A floorboard creaked in the Bicks' room, and as she approached, Meaghan came out with her basket of cleaning supplies and an armload of crumpled towels.

The other girl's eyes widened. "You startled me."

Landon matched her low tone. "Sorry. Is Anna lying down?"

"She said to raid the fridge if you get hungry. She wants to be back on her feet before the guests come back. I just need to put everything away, and then I'm done."

"Your ride is waiting."

Meaghan's breath hissed. "I'm later than I thought." But she didn't seem to hurry on the stairs. "I'm off tomorrow. See you Monday. Good luck."
~~~

Landon unlocked her room and flopped on the bed. Her phone had buzzed an email alert while she was talking to Meaghan. She opened a new message from her prof.

Keep pace with the course load. We cover too much ground for you to try playing catch-up. I expect you back as soon as possible.

The words conjured her crisp voice and determined face, warning students on day one that they were adults and would not be coddled.

Landon rested the phone on her stomach and stared up at the slanted ceiling. "As soon as possible" had better be quick. She had to either confirm the prowler was real, or prove he wasn't—and convince Anna to seek help.

She climbed off the bed and picked up her laptop. Working in the kitchen would let her hear when Anna got up. They had to talk.

At least this prof was progressive enough to choose material available in electronic format. Digital books still cost a fortune, but they made this trip a lot lighter. Another benefit of e-textbooks was the text-to-speech software. Bouncing between that and reading, she focused better and for longer. Still, by the time Anna's door opened, Landon's brain felt like a pincushion.

Anna's face had lost its pinched look. The nap must have helped.

"Feeling better?"

"Pretty much. Did you find something to eat?"

"I grabbed an apple."

"I'll make us some sandwiches." Anna trailed a hand across Landon's shoulder as she passed. "It's so good to have you here, even for a bit."

When they finished eating, Landon slid her plate to the side and opened her laptop. She started a blank document. "If I'm going to help, I need to know everything that's happened. When did the trouble start?"

Anna frowned, and glanced toward the wall calendar.

"Maybe two weeks now? I'd heard whistling outside my window late at night, a few times, and couldn't see anyone."

She tucked her hair behind an ear. "He never leaves a trace. I was starting to worry about myself, but that Friday—no, it was Thursday—I did see him. He stood by the garden, facing the inn, but by the time I reached the kitchen to turn on the outside light, he was gone."

Landon typed "Whistling. Garden." Not much, so far. She looked at Anna. "And you couldn't identify him?"

"He always wears dark clothes, and a hat or a hoodie. And it's dark at night out here in the country."

"What about leaving your outside light on?"

Anna's mouth turned down. "I tried that. He stayed outside the circle of the light and that made it harder to see him."

"That's why you have the big flashlight?"

"Not that it's helped."

"Okay, so what has he done since then?"

Anna lifted the tea cozy off the pot and poured herself another cup. "More of the same. Different sounds, sometimes, and I don't always see him. And he plays little tricks, like sticking my clogs where I'd trip on them, the day you came."

Unless Anna had left them in the way, herself. Landon started a new column for tricks. She added "Clogs," and looked at Anna. "What else?"

Anna's eyebrows scrunched. "It's simple things. Like opening the patio umbrella on the deck after I've closed it. Putting the chair pads back on, when they were in the big rubber tote out there. Unfastening the garbage can so the raccoons can get in."

The phone cut her off. She plucked the handset from the shelf. "Hello, Green Dory Inn."

With a huff, she set the phone back in its charger and turned back to Landon. "I can't blame him for the telemarketers, but it's tempting."

"Just don't pick up."

Anna sat heavily enough to squeak her chair legs on the floor. "An unknown name could be a person on a cell, wanting a reservation. I do ignore the toll-frees."

They finished Anna's list of pranks, and it left Landon with an uneasy feeling in her stomach. These were all things Anna might have done herself. Everybody had lapses like this. But so many in such a short time...

"So he's never done anything destructive, or that you could prove?"

Anna propped her elbows on the table and dropped her chin into her hands. "I almost wish he did. Then people would believe me."

The resignation in her eyes said she knew Landon had doubts.

Landon closed the laptop. "I'll keep watch tonight. If I can see him too, you have your proof."

She'd used her most confident tone, but what-ifs whispered in her mind.

The lines edging Anna's eyes didn't soften. "He doesn't come every night. Still, if you stay on my couch again, I'll be smart enough to wake you this time if I hear anything."

A shiver brushed the back of Landon's neck. She'd slept through the night after Anna's fright, but woke with a dull soul-ache that said her dreams had touched some very dark places.

She hugged her arms around her midriff. "I don't know if I'll be able to sleep anyway."

Chapter 4

Sunday

LANDON WAS CHOPPING tomatoes for a salad the next day when Anna returned from church.

Anna set her bag beside the door and squeezed her in a one-armed hug. "Thanks again for covering for me. I wish there was an evening service for those of us who work in the mornings. I assume the Bicks' check-out went okay?"

"They said they'll leave a good review online."

Anna's smile didn't spread as wide as usual. "They wouldn't if they'd heard me scream Friday night. I need this prowler business settled before it starts affecting the guests."

And before the strain of being back here made Landon fall apart. She turned back to the cutting board. The past was behind her. She couldn't let it undo her again.

Somehow she had to help end this. See Anna's prowler or disprove him.

There'd been no suspicious activity overnight. Only another tortured dream. Her thrashing had wakened Anna and earned a baleful look from Timkin.

She dumped the tomato pieces into the bowl of greens and reached for the freshly-scrubbed mushrooms. "I know you've already gone over the property, but let's look again. We might find something."

"We can try, but he's good at covering his tracks."

Anna pulled out plates and set them on the table. "I wish you could have come with me this morning. Some of the congregation would remember you, and they'd be so glad to see you doing well."

The knife gouged a wedge out of the mushroom Landon held and thunked into the cutting board.

The church people who knew her would have prayed when she disappeared. Landon owed them her thanks. But that first encounter was always awkward. Sympathy and concern saw her as the victim she'd been, not the survivor she was today.

She gripped the knife more carefully and made slow, deliberate slices. "Anna, it's true what they say—sometimes you can't go home again."

Although Roy hadn't made it awkward.

She carried the salad bowl to the table and sat facing Anna. Roy was an exception. She forced a brighter tone. "I listened to a podcast message and some worship music, and had my own prayer time on the deck."

They were clearing up after lunch when a knock came at the back door. Anna hurried to answer.

Landon picked out a male voice. It didn't sound like the constable, or like Roy or Bobby.

A minute later, Anna came back. "Come meet Meaghan's dad. He moved home a few years ago." She dropped her tone. "He was a lot like Quinn when he was young, but he grew out of it."

Landon followed her into the sitting room. With no paying guests, the entire inn was theirs to use, but Anna seemed to prefer to keep to her own living quarters.

A pale man in a tan golf shirt and sharp-creased trousers stood from the couch and extended his hand to Landon. "Gord Lohnes. Pleased to meet you."

He sank back into his seat.

Landon skirted the coffee table and settled in the second

recliner. Meaghan's father could be about Anna's age, maybe a bit older, but the years had taken more of a toll. His skin had a pasty look, and his body didn't quite fill his clothes.

Gord declined Anna's offer of a drink. "I can't stay long. I'm on my way to Halifax for a few days. Cardiologist appointment first thing in the morning, and I have some things to take care of."

He leaned forward in his seat, gaze locked on Anna. "Meaghan told me you had another incident Friday night. You deserve better than this. Let me buy the inn."

At Anna's cry of protest, he spread his hands. "Don't answer today, but think about it while I'm gone. This anxiety's too hard on you, especially when you've lost your husband."

Anna's open face took on a set expression Landon hadn't seen often. "Gord, I appreciate your kindness, but—"

"I know. Just let it brew a bit. I'll call when I'm home." He pushed up from the couch, his smile enveloping them both. "Enjoy your stay, Landon. And keep an eye on Anna for us."

Once Anna closed the door behind him, she seemed to deflate. "He doesn't understand. The inn was Murdoch's dream. Letting it go would mean losing the only part of him I have left."

She swiped the tears from her eyes and straightened her shoulders. "And whatever it takes, that's not going to happen."

Landon nodded, not breaking eye contact. "Then let's hunt for clues."

They spent at least an hour combing the grounds and the woods. The trees had been thinned long ago, and they'd grown straight and tall. Murdoch, or someone before him, had cut out the underbrush and left easy walking under the green canopy.

A fair distance behind the inn, the growth became more tangled at the property line. It stayed open in both directions toward the neighbouring homes. A person could travel quite a way before cutting out to the road, and this far in, nobody would notice.

Landon scuffed her shoe into the moss on an old stump. She had to concede there was nothing to see. Rusty fallen pine needles and packed dirt hid any tracks under the trees, and if a prowler had travelled this way, he'd been careful not to drop anything.

Anna picked up a dead branch and tossed it aside. "He most likely comes through the trees, but I don't see how that helps us. Give me half an hour to lie down, and then let's go play tourist. It's not right for my problems to be taking over your life."

Anna's problems were the whole reason Landon was here, jeopardizing her studies and her mental health. She opened her mouth to object, then shut it again. Staying here would let Anna brood over the lack of evidence—and Gord's offer to buy the inn. As kind as he seemed, couldn't he see how much of Anna's heart was invested in this place?

Landon's school work would have to wait. "A change of scene might clear our minds."

"How about we pack a picnic supper and head out to The Ovens?"

Excitement sparked, for the first time since she'd returned. As a child, she'd found the park's sea caves to be places of wonder.

They came back tired from hiking in the fresh air, with their stress at least temporarily washed away.

After a quiet evening that brought her no new ideas, Landon decided to stay on Anna's couch again that night. They didn't have to worry about disturbing guests, but she needed to hear if Anna called. "He knows which room is yours, and this is where he's targeting. I want to see him."

"If he shows up." Anna folded her knitting and put it away. "I'm going to get some sleep. Here's hoping we don't talk again until morning."

"Good night." Landon repositioned her laptop on her

knees and went back to work.

Keeping up with the readings and writing her paper she could do, but things might come up in class discussions that she'd need on the final.

If she made it home for the final. She couldn't ask Roy for another ticket back here afterwards, and she couldn't leave Anna alone if this wasn't solved.

No evidence, no witnesses... A queasy sensation filled her stomach. Anna was carrying so much. Losing her life partner in a car crash, trying to continue his legacy with Corey, running the inn alone.

People's minds played crazy tricks sometimes, if the pressure built too high. The inn was all Anna had left of her husband. Her prowler could be a projection of her fear of losing that, too.

Acid burbled in Landon's stomach. They had to both see this guy. Anna would be devastated if this was all in her head.

She forced her attention back to her work. An hour later, eyes burning, she closed the laptop and slid it under the couch.

Timkin blinked at her from Anna's chair.

"You want to go out before I lie down?"

The cat dropped his head back onto his paws and shut his eyes.

Landon went upstairs to get ready for bed. After hiking and homework, maybe she'd sleep without dreams.

When she turned out the light to go back downstairs, she waited in the darkness until her eyes adjusted, then surveyed the back yard. As she turned away, she thought she spotted movement.

Frozen in place, she let her vision lose focus, open to pick up any sign of motion. Nothing.

Then a large shadow detached from the trees. Landon caught her breath. Anna's prowler.

Or... a deer. The animal walked toward the garden and lowered its head. So that's what had been eating the flowers.

Landon's heartbeat slowed. For a second, she'd thought this was proof of Anna's claims.

Suddenly the deer straightened, ears tall. One flip of its white tail, and it bounded into the forest.

Something must have spooked it. Probably another animal, but what if—

A dark-clad figure stepped around the driveway side of the house.

Landon's breath hissed. How could she have doubted Anna?

"Please don't be Corey again, or someone else looking out for Anna." She whipped out her phone and connected with a 9-1-1 operator.

The intruder below stood still, as if listening.

Landon hurried through the dim house and down the stairs while she told the operator what she'd seen. "He hasn't done anything yet tonight, but last time he tapped on my friend's window and scared her."

In the kitchen, she sneaked to the window. "I don't see him anymore. I'll check another window."

Nothing from Anna's sitting room. Landon picked her way around the furniture to check the windows on both sides. Had he climbed to Anna's again? Quiet snores drifted from the bedroom. She crept in, checked outside, and went back to the kitchen before speaking again. "I'll look on the other sides of the house."

After the final window, she slumped into a chair. "I think he's gone. There's no point sending anyone now."

"Well, keep a lookout, and if you need us, call back right away. I'll log this for an officer to follow up in the morning." With an encouragement to stay safe, the operator ended the connection.

Landon leaned her head against the chair back and stared at the darkened ceiling. In ordinary circumstances, a vanishing prowler would be a relief. Not a let-down.

She'd been so close to vindicating Anna's stories. But

Anna's prowler always made sure she knew he was there. This guy left her alone.

Maybe he was just a random trespasser.

If Anna's prowler was only a subconscious cry for help, the reassurance of Landon's continued presence could make him unnecessary.

Landon groaned. She couldn't stay here forever.

Chapter 5

Monday

NO GUESTS MEANT a later start to Monday morning. Landon waited until she and Anna finished breakfast to bring up what happened in the night. “They’re sending a patrol car this morning. The dispatcher agreed it could wait for daylight.”

Anna tapped her fingernails on the side of her tea mug. “They won’t find anything, but at least now you’ve seen him too.”

If it was the same man. Heat prickled Landon’s hairline at the thought. “Why didn’t he wake you?”

“I was pretty tired. Maybe he tried and gave up.”

“Maybe.” Landon stacked their dishes and carried them to the sink.

They had to both see this guy, together, or she had to see nothing when Anna pointed him out. Either way, they could take the next step. This waiting was getting them nowhere.

The growl of a car engine drew her gaze outside.

Meaghan’s car pulled into the lot, and she stepped out of the passenger side. She hadn’t taken more than two steps before her boyfriend reversed the car and pointed it back toward the road. He stopped and glared at the inn before speeding down the driveway.

A shiver trickled across the back of Landon's neck. That man had serious hostility issues.

Meaghan opened the door with a quiet "Hello." Whatever his attitude, or maybe because of it, she seemed to relax as she stepped into the inn's sunny kitchen.

"Good morning." Anna's chair scraped back from the table. After some friendly chat, she said, "We have a reservation tonight, and they wanted an early check-in. They should be here before noon. I'm going to get started on some pumpkin-spice muffins."

"Which room will they have?"

"I put them in the Schooner room."

"I'll make sure it's ready before I change out Saturday's room."

Landon wandered out to the garden to snip fresh flowers for the tables. It had rained sometime in the night, and the wet grass soaked the canvas toes of her shoes. Water pooled in the twin-pointed hoof prints where the deer had stopped to feed.

She chose some vibrant blue blooms. A few yellow ones from the inn's namesake dory would add variety.

Walking along the driveway toward the dory in front of the house, she scanned the ground for traces of the intruder. Nothing.

She'd seen him at this side of the building, not the rear where Anna said he usually appeared. That was another odd thing, although for all she knew he'd circled the inn a few times before being spotted.

Fist full of flowers, she was heading back along the driveway when the purr of an engine crept up behind her. She stepped to the edge of the pavement and looked around.

The police, as promised. The car pulled ahead and parked beside Anna's. Constable Tremblay smiled as he joined Landon at the slate path that led to the deck.

"We have to stop meeting like this." He gestured for her to precede him along the path.

Anna came outside to meet them. "Dylan, do you ever get a day off?"

"One or two."

He surveyed the property. "Report says Ms. Smith called this one in, but the person didn't stick around. Did you both see him?"

"No."

"So we don't know if it's the same individual you've seen, Anna, or someone just passing through."

Landon twisted her hair into a rope. He didn't believe Anna either. No evidence, no witnesses... no wonder they doubted.

"I was watching a deer, and something startled it. Then he came around the corner of the house." She pointed.

Constable Tremblay gestured at the flowers in her hand. "You've been walking around already. Have you noticed anything?"

"No. And I've been careful to look where I was going, so I wouldn't mess up any clues." She sighed. "There aren't any."

He slid his notepad and pen into a pocket. "Let me widen the perimeter."

Landon and Anna retreated to the deck while he walked an increasing spiral around the back yard.

After he'd worked through the edge of the forest and gone up and down the driveway, he mounted the steps to join them. "Your deer left the only traces. All I can do is remind you to keep a lookout. And remember, do not engage if you see him."

Another car pulled into the lot and parked beside the police cruiser.

Anna sighed. "No offence, Dylan, but I hoped you'd be gone before our guests arrived."

Landon watched her stroll toward the car. Nobody would know from her body language that the inn's hostess was close to cracking.

A tall, silver-haired man climbed from the vehicle and

stepped around to open the door for his passenger. The woman stood as far on the short side of average as his height put him above it, with soft brown curls and a flowing jade blouse over tan capris. Clutching the man's hand, she backed away from the cruiser, eyes wide.

Anna's voice carried to the deck. "Welcome. You must be the Livingstones. I'm Anna Young. Let me take you around to the entrance, and we'll get you settled."

Mrs. Livingstone stood still. "What's wrong?"

Constable Tremblay lifted his eyebrows at Landon. "Guess I'd better go and make some peace."

Landon followed him along the path and gave the newcomers her friendliest smile. *Nothing to worry about here, folks. Enjoy your stay, but don't look out the windows after dark.*

The officer extended his hand to Mr. Livingstone and then to his wife. "Constable Tremblay. Welcome to Lunenburg, folks. There's no cause for alarm. I'm following up on a report of a trespasser overnight. The individual must have been just passing through. We've had no indication of anything you need to concern yourselves with."

Mrs. Livingstone looked up at her husband. "We can't stay here, George. I won't rest at all."

"The officer said it's perfectly safe, dear."

"He can't guarantee that. Please, take me somewhere else."

The tall man's eyes were apologetic. "Unfortunately we'll need to cancel, Ms. Young. I'm sure we'd have been most comfortable here, but my wife's nerves are delicate, and this is meant to be a relaxing getaway."

Anna's smile didn't slip. "I understand. Let me recommend another spot. It's nearer town, so you might feel more secure."

Mrs. Livingstone gave a tentative nod, and Anna said, "I'll phone to see if they have a vacancy."

As the Livingstones drove away, Anna's smile crumbled.

"It was bad enough for him to sneak around after dark and frighten me, but I knew this would happen. He's affecting the inn."

Landon slid her arms around her and squeezed. "We'll find out what's going on. It'll be okay. Besides, Mrs. L. seemed pretty high-maintenance. You might be better off without them."

Constable Tremblay picked up a flower lying on the driveway, and handed the limp bloom to Landon. "This escaped your bouquet."

He angled his face toward Anna. "I'm sorry we didn't find anything, but don't let it get you down. You have a beautiful spot here, and I'll try not to scare anyone else away."

"You don't believe last night's sighting was the same man who's been bothering me."

One of his eyelids twitched. "Belief doesn't matter. We need facts."

Anna's cheeks reddened. She looked from him to Landon. "I am not going crazy."

Landon took her hand. "Anna... we have to find out what's happening. If it were a mental health issue, wouldn't you want to know? To get help?"

"But I saw him. I heard him scrape at my window screen."

"And the guy I saw didn't try to bother you at all." The words tore Landon's heart, but she couldn't ignore that truth. If he'd wanted to wake Anna and had circled the building, he'd have tried one last time at her window before leaving.

The hurt look on Anna's face made her feel hollow inside. "We'll keep watching. If we both see him, that's the proof we need."

Anna's eyes pinched at the corners. "And if only I see him..."

"I'll be here for you while we find out why." Landon kept hold of her hand. "Thank you for everything, Constable."

"Call me Dylan. We're pretty informal around here. And Anna, I care too. Stay strong." Half-way to his cruiser, he turned. "Oh—your car window's down, and it rained overnight."

"I always close them. You know what the flies are like around here."

He lifted a shoulder. "It didn't look like much water blew in. Probably be dry by mid-afternoon."

Anna walked over to her car and frowned at the open driver's window. "I know I closed it."

She grabbed the door handle and pulled. When it opened, she turned troubled eyes on the officer. "I locked it, too."

Landon tried the passenger door. Locked. Like she'd left it last night. She looked over the car roof at Dylan.

The stiff set of his mouth said he didn't want to argue, but he took an audible breath and stepped toward Anna. "You've been under a lot of stress. These things happen."

They'd been out last night. Landon replayed their movements in her mind. She wouldn't have noticed if Anna closed the window—except for the hornet.

She rapped her knuckles on the roof. "The window was up."

They both stared at her. Dylan's posture stayed the same, but Anna's expression softened, and she seemed to relax.

Landon wanted to shout for joy. Yes, Anna had a prowler to deal with, but she was okay. Mentally, she was okay.

How could they have been so quick to doubt her? She grinned at Dylan. "When we came back last night, Anna had just rolled up her window when a big hornet bounced off it. We joked about how if it had hit the side of her head, there'd be a dent."

Anna's shoulders straightened. "That's right."

Dylan looked from one to the other. "You're sure that was last night?"

Landon was practically vibrating with happiness. Anna was okay. "Positive. It's the only time I've been in the car. And they're manual windows—easy for him to open once he broke in."

The notebook was back in Dylan's hand. After jotting a few notes, he pulled out his phone and snapped some photos. He studied the car door, running a finger along the rubber sheath that held the window. Activating the phone's flashlight app, he peered under the car.

Landon and Anna stood back and watched him work.

Eventually he made another circuit around the vehicle and joined them. "My initial check didn't show anything, and by now we've likely destroyed any fingerprints. Do you need to go anywhere today?"

"Nowhere that can't wait." Anna sounded more secure, but there was no "I told you so" in her tone or on her face—just a calm that had been missing since Landon arrived.

"Good. I'd like to have this checked for prints, just in case. We might get a partial from the window handle, or he may have braced his hand against the roof when he popped the lock. But prints or no, we have our first bit of circumstantial evidence."

Landon still held the flowers for the tables. She tapped the blossoms against her leg. "He worked so hard not to leave any trace. What changed?"

Dylan put his phone away. "It may turn out to be an unrelated prank, but assuming it's our guy, it does fit the pattern of someone who's trying to unsettle Anna. If you hadn't seen him—and corroborated the closed window—it would be one more thing to cast doubt on her."

"But he's escalating. Are we in danger?"

Dylan's eyes narrowed, as if he were assessing the risk. He looked at Anna, then back at Landon. "My gut says no. Not at this point."

Landon shivered. They had to catch him before it reached the point where it did get dangerous.

He didn't seem to notice her reaction. "You both know there are no guarantees. These have all been mischief offences, though. Nothing threatening."

He pointed his notebook at Anna. "No trying to engage

him. He could turn violent if he were cornered. Let us do our job."

As if random drive-by patrols would spot a prowler who slunk through the woods. Landon gave her head a little shake. Surely the police would do more than that. This wasn't their first intruder case. Still, she and Anna had a more personal sense of urgency about it all.

Anna might have read her mind. "My business is still at stake, and Landon has to get back to school."

He turned to Landon, his brown eyes friendly. "Where do you teach?"

"I'm a student. It's a university course."

"Well, we'll try to free you up as fast as we can—and avoid scaring off any more of Anna's reservations in the meantime."

Landon glanced at the car. "I keep wondering about Quinn."

"I haven't caught up with him yet for a chat, but I think if he wanted to lash out, there'd be spray paint on the buildings or a rock through the windshield. Although I'm sure he has the necessary skill to have popped the car lock."

Dylan slid his notebook back into his pocket. "I'll talk to him."

He made eye contact with each of them in turn. "Keep watch, and try not to worry. Now, I'd better get out of here before another guest shows up."

Landon stared after his departing car and then turned to face Anna. "I'm sorry I doubted you. I felt—well, like I had to face all the possibilities, no matter how horrible."

"You were right, even if I didn't want to hear it. I am so glad to know it's not me."

"Me, too. Now we have to find out who it really is."

Anna headed for the inn. "You heard Dylan. It's not a job for civilians."

Landon caught up and shot her a look. "Has that ever stopped you helping someone before? This time, the person you're helping is you."

As soon as the back door closed behind them, feet pounded down the stairs from the guest rooms. Meaghan scurried up to Anna, eyes wide. "What's happened now? I saw the police car."

"Something good, for a change. Our prowler broke into my car overnight and put the window down for some kind of prank. He didn't know I'd have a witness who remembered me putting it up." She flashed Landon a satisfied look. "They'll have to take me seriously now."

She turned back to Meaghan. "But Dylan being here scared away our reservation for tonight."

"Oh, no." Meaghan bit her lower lip, her gaze darting around the room. "If it gets worse, it could make you close the inn."

Anna took her hand. "We have to believe they'll catch this guy, and he's never targeted the guests. Please don't worry, Meaghan. Your job's safe."

The assurance didn't match Anna's reaction when the Livingstones had left. Landon pressed her lips shut and held back a sigh. Anna could hold it together for everyone around her, but the fear was still there inside, undermining and fermenting, despite her faith.

Meaghan's eyes filled. "You're so kind. This shouldn't be happening. I have to finish up before Hart gets here." She pulled her hand free of Anna's grasp and fled.

Landon scowled. "You're sure that guy's not hurting her? He can't even let her come to work on her own."

"He has a second job making deliveries, or something. When he's not at the plant, he needs the car." Anna's lips turned down. "He's unpleasant, and Meaghan's troubled, but I don't think that's why. She hasn't opened up to me yet."

"She will."

A muffin pan, filled with orange-brown batter, sat beside the stove. Anna slid it into the oven. "This is definitely pre-heated by now. Good thing I didn't stick them in before I went outside."

"There'll be more for us, without the Livingstones." Landon remembered sharing muffins and tea with their strange visitor. "Does Nigel roam through the woods a lot?"

"Is he back again?"

She peeked out the window. "No, but could you ask him to pay extra attention around your property and watch for clues? He seems like he'd notice things out of place."

Anna's chuckle was fond. "That he does, although our prowler hasn't left any traces yet."

"But you'll phone him and ask?"

Anna took a scrub brush to the mixing bowl soaking in the sink. "Nigel won't use the phone. He thinks the aliens can record it, and he's not giving them his voice." She glanced at Landon. "His words, not mine. I'll call his mother and leave a message."

"Has he always been like this?" Adults could be cruel enough. School must have been torture for him. It had been horrible for Landon at the end, and she hadn't stood out that much.

The bowl clunked into the dishwasher rack. Anna straightened, and dried her hands. "I didn't meet him until we moved here, but there were stories. I don't think he's changed much. Beneath the quirks, he's a lovely man."

"I'm sure your acceptance means a lot."

Landon snipped the shrivelled ends off the flower stems and filled the table vases at the counter by the sink. "I hope these will last."

"Pansies are sturdy. They'll be fine."

Anna was sturdy, too, but the stress and loss of sleep were affecting her.

Landon picked up two of the vases. "If this guy's going to be sneaking around causing trouble, let's string some dark thread between the trees. When he breaks it, we'll at least have an angle of approach. Plus you need motion-sensor lights."

Anna shook her head. "Motion sensors won't work. We're in the country. We have nocturnal wildlife."

She took the other two vases and carried them toward the eating area.

"We also have a nocturnal prowler. And we need to know what he's up to." Landon positioned the flowers on the tables, admiring their cheerful blooms. Good thing the deer didn't eat the whole garden.

Garden. Gardening clogs.

She spun to look at Anna. "He's been coming in the daytime too. That explains your clogs being where you'd trip on them. Things like the garbage lid could have been done during the day, too. You don't just need lights. You need cameras."

Anna's mouth twitched like she'd swallowed something unpleasant. "I can't have all that. What would the guests think?"

"Most people won't notice, and those who do should be glad you're providing security for their vehicles."

A slow breath said Anna wasn't convinced. "I need to go clear the Livingstones' reservation from my bookings in case someone else wants that room."

Landon followed her into her sitting room. Timkin yawned at them from the couch, and Landon sat beside him, stroking his soft fur while Anna adjusted her website.

"Anna, we have to do this. I know he keeps his head covered, but a video would show his size, the way he walks, and maybe catch his face. Your inn's worth fighting for, so let's fight."

Her hand stilled on Timkin's back and she grinned. "How's your aim? We could nail him with a paintball gun, and give the police some evidence."

Anna snorted, but her smile stretched wide enough to crinkle the corners of her eyes. "I couldn't even hit the proverbial broad side of my own barn. You?"

"Not a chance. I'll bet Roy could, though."

"Oh, there's plenty of mischief in that one. If his leg was better, he'd be all over the idea."

She turned off the computer monitor. "You're right. I'll leave a message for Nigel and then see if Roy will lend us his truck, since I told Dylan the car would be here for them to check. We can get the cameras, and pick up whatever you didn't pack for the weekend."

It would be a definite improvement not to be tied to the washing machine. "I just hope we don't meet anyone who'll know me."

Anna's lips didn't move, but her face said to let it go.

Landon held her gaze. "It's just—uncomfortable. And easier if we avoid it."

While Anna made her calls, Landon tied light brown thread from tree to tree a few feet into the forest. With a daytime prowler in mind, she didn't dare put it as high as she'd like, but hopefully he wouldn't notice the blending colour at ankle height. A chipmunk or red squirrel would fit underneath, but a rabbit or bigger animal could break it as well as a human. She and Anna wouldn't know the difference.

She took the nearly-empty spool back inside to Anna. "Did you mention the thread to Nigel's mother?"

"She'll tell him to watch for it."

Ten minutes later, they rattled toward town in Roy's truck, Landon in a borrowed ball cap with the brim pulled low. When they struck out locally, they drove to nearby Bridgewater. As well as picking up the items Landon needed for a longer stay, they hit every hardware store in town. Nobody stocked motion-sensor cameras. Lights, yes, but cameras were a special order.

It was late afternoon before they returned the truck and collapsed into chairs on the inn's back deck.

"At least we'll have extra lights tonight." Landon kicked off her shoes and flexed her toes against the wooden decking.

Eyes closed, Anna massaged her forehead. "They'll

probably turn on every time a rabbit hops past. Or that deer that thinks my garden's a buffet."

Not something city dwellers had to worry about. But if this helped stop the prowler, it'd be worth some false alarms.

After a few minutes of surfing the web for security cameras, Landon handed her phone to Anna. "This is the best-looking option I found. It'll send your phone a push notification whenever it detects movement, so we can see what we've got."

Anna squinted at the screen. "You mean besides the wildlife? I have to get an electrician in to install the lights, and unless he has a better suggestion, I'll order these."

She returned the phone. "Willy's a good friend and a good worker, but he's a talker. Everyone will know we're getting new security features… and why."

"That could be a bonus. Maybe your visitor will go bother someone else."

Timkin wandered up the stairs from the grass and jumped onto Anna's lap. Stroking his back, she winked at Landon. "Looks like you're on supper duty. It'd be cruel to move him."

"Well played." Landon stood. "Did you let your other neighbours know about the car break-in? Just in case this guy decides to widen his field?"

"So far he's targeting me, but you're right. I'll do that as soon as I reach Willy."

"What if he's busy tonight?

A sad smile tugged at Anna's lips. "He's been so helpful since I lost Murdoch. He'll squeeze in the time."

After they ate, while Anna cleaned up, Landon curled up in the sitting room with her laptop. She hadn't planned on a whole day without any course work, and the way she felt now, there'd be no brain power left by the time the electrician had come and gone.

Timkin leaped onto the couch and blinked at her.

"Sorry, cat. This lap's full." She checked the course syllabus, and opened the next reading. No point turning on the text-to-speech software. After shopping with Anna until they'd nearly dropped, the flat voice would have her asleep in no time.

Instead, she read the same few paragraphs at least five times before groaning and snapping the laptop shut. Timkin opened one eye at the sound.

She had to do this. Had to focus, read, learn, but her mind refused—even while her thoughts were churning up an anxiety cloud in her chest.

Summer courses spread the load so she could carry less during the rest of the year. This one was a prerequisite for next month's work with the same professor. She had to do more than just pass. If she didn't score high enough to meet the entry requirement, she'd have to repeat in September, instead of finding her first co-op work placement.

Anna wouldn't want her to jeopardize her studies. It would be safer to go home. Escape the nightmares and put school first.

They knew the prowler was real, now, not a product of Anna's imagination. He didn't seem dangerous, and Anna wouldn't be afraid to stay alone.

Landon put her laptop aside and slid closer to Timkin, who didn't even twitch. His soft fur under her fingertips soothed her, and the repetitive stroking motion helped her think.

Leaving now would be running away, failing Anna in her time of need. She'd meant what she said about fighting for the inn, and Anna seemed too worn down by the stress to do that on her own.

Together, they had a better chance.

As for today, with the excitement of proving this prowler to be real, and the tiredness from shopping so long after a troubled night, no wonder she couldn't force herself to study.

She ran a knuckle along Timkin's head between his ears, and along the curve of his back. Time to stop pressuring herself and recharge a bit. Maybe she could work later tonight after all. If not, first thing in the morning.

When she stood, Timkin gave a lazy yawn and jumped down from the couch. Landon followed him to the door, let him out, then went in search of Anna.

She found her friend settled in one of the inn's Adirondack chairs on the front lawn, watching a few sailboats glide across the water. Landon dropped into the chair beside her. "I'm beat."

"We'll sleep well tonight. If the lights don't keep waking us."

They sat in silence until a silver pickup rattled into the yard, "Willy's Wiring" on the door.

Willy's size and his wrinkled face made him look like he'd shrunk in the wash. A thick crop of white hair, and bright blue eyes, proved his vitality hadn't faded.

When Anna introduced them, his wide grin and warm, double-fisted hand-clasp won Landon's heart.

Landon squeezed back. "I'm glad Anna has such good friends."

"No more than she deserves. We'll all be glad to see this nuisance caught."

"Nobody has any idea who it could be?"

"None. And I keep my ears open."

Willy followed them around the back and through the back door to where Anna had stacked the lights. He opened the boxes and checked the contents, chatting non-stop until he carried his work back outside.

Anna's smile carried strain. "See what I meant?"

She sat at the kitchen table and dropped her chin into her hands.

Landon made her a cup of tea while Willy bumped and clattered outside. Once he'd finished the interior connections, he visited a bit longer and took off "home to the Missus."

Half an hour later, Landon found Anna in the private sitting room, facing a blank computer screen. "Hey, is something wrong?"

"I went online and ordered the cameras."

Landon knelt beside her and took her hand. "But what?"

A tear slipped down Anna's cheek. "That was a simple job, tonight. Murdoch could have done it. But he's gone." Her face crumpled.

Landon rose to a half-crouch and pulled her into a tight embrace. "It's the little things, isn't it?"

Anna's head nodded against her shoulder. "God is good, but this is so hard."

Landon's throat tightened. Her mother had gone through this too, without knowing the Lord's comfort, and with only Landon's younger sisters to help. No wonder she'd turned bitter.

Shoving that tangled ache back into hiding, Landon focused on the present. She was here, now, with Anna. She couldn't ease the loss of a good husband, but she could help end the prowler's torment.

Somehow.

Chapter 6

Tuesday

The alarm on her phone nagged Landon into a muzzy consciousness. She groaned and sat up in bed before she could sink back into sleep. Legs criss-cross, she stretched forward between her knees and then straightened, breathing in and holding it until her chest strained.

Knowing the prowler was real meant she hadn't needed to camp on Anna's couch to be sure they both saw him. Even a single bed would have been a step up, and this queen-sized one was pure luxury.

Landon swung her feet over the side. Her dreams had not been good. Even though she'd slept through them, the battered feeling in her spirit was evidence of the struggle.

She'd left her curtains open, but the lights had only woken her once, for a raccoon. A big one. If their human nuisance had come slinking around and Anna saw him, they might have information for the police. If they were lucky, the lights would scare him off for good.

Maybe they should post photos of the security fixtures on Anna's social media. And tag them #prowler #stayaway.

Anna wasn't in the kitchen when she came downstairs, but Timkin appeared from wherever he'd been lurking. He mewed twice and strolled to the back door.

Landon clicked the deadbolt and followed him outside into a refreshingly cool morning. She scanned the trees. None of her threads were visible, but that was the point.

Anna's gardening clogs lay neatly by the railing. Landon slid them on and clomped down the stairs to the grass. The fresh forest scent lifted her spirits, and she dawdled along the tree line, inhaling the tangy air and listening to the chatter of birds.

The second-last thread trailed on the ground, broken ends fluttering in the breeze. Of course there was nothing else to see.

Above her, a squirrel scolded. She finally spotted the little rust-coloured animal hunkered on a high branch. "Too bad we couldn't train you guys as sentinels."

"They're always watching, but don't trust them."

Landon shrieked and spun into a defensive stance.

Nigel Foley jumped back, blinking rapidly. He clutched his metal detector across his chest like a shield. "Are any other lines breached too?"

She shook her head, gasping for breath. "Just this one. Please—never sneak up on me again."

He regarded her in utter seriousness. "I stepped heavier so you'd hear."

The squirrel made a chuckling sound. Landon glared upward as it leaped onto a connecting branch and streaked down the tree trunk. It raced away.

The inn door banged. "Did you find something?" Anna crossed the deck to the railing.

Nigel loped toward the building. His scuffed army boots made no sound, on the forest floor or the grass, and he moved with a fluidity at odds with his disjointed mannerisms.

Landon's pulse still hadn't recovered from fight-or-flight mode. She took another steadying breath and started back to the inn. Nigel Foley was exactly who they needed to patrol these woods.

When Anna heard about the broken thread, she glanced

at Landon. “Did you see anyone last night? A raccoon roamed through, and our deer came back.”

“I missed the deer.” She set Anna’s clogs back where she’d found them. “I suppose an animal broke the thread. Our guy could have come before dark, but he’d have caused some mischief, and everything looks fine.”

“That one was down yesterday afternoon.” Nigel mashed his camouflage hat more firmly onto his head, making his hair stick out around it. “Mother gave me your message, but you were gone when I came. Your screen door was flapping, so I shut it.”

Anna’s eyes narrowed, and her lips thinned into a line.

The inside door stood open. After checking the lock, Anna shook her head. “I don’t see any scratches like he was trying to get in. I’ll report it, but it’s probably another of his little tricks to make me think I’m losing it.”

The screen door only locked from the inside, if at all. Anna had been the last out when they’d left to go shopping. If they didn’t know the prowler was real, Landon could have believed she forgot to close it.

With this guy coming during the day as well as after dark, maybe they should park Anna’s car at Roy’s, and sneak back to keep watch. It could be a long wait, but if the cameras didn’t come soon, they might have to try it.

Landon turned to Nigel. “So could you walk through a little more often? I’ll keep a better eye on the trip-lines, but we need someone to actually see this guy. Or to find a clue, if he ever drops one.”

A sly grin appeared on his face, and he gave three rapid nods. “Stealth is key.”

She studied the line of trees behind the inn. To the left lay Roy’s house. “What’s directly behind us, Anna? Besides trees? And who lives to the right, with our broken thread?”

“The woods go back for a couple of miles. Next door’s vacant, and I know the next few neighbours. Elva Knapp’s a single lady. She doesn’t like there being an inn here, but she'd hardly be sneaking through the woods in the middle of the night. Past her are my friend Tricia and her husband. Quinn's staying with them, but like Dylan said, this isn't destructive enough to be him."

Landon was picturing the "for sale" sign they'd passed yesterday. From the road, the empty house had looked in good shape, and about the same size as the Green Dory. "If Meaghan's father really wants to live in this area, why not buy the place next door?"

"It's this one he wants. A childhood friend lived here, and I guess Gord had more happy moments here than he did at home."

A scowl chased across Nigel Foley's face. He hefted his metal detector. "I'll report in when I can. Better be on my way."

Anna reached for the door handle. "No time to visit today, Nigel?"

He shook his head and made a funny half-bow before he left.

Landon followed her inside. Time for breakfast. And for some brainstorming, before the spark of excitement died and she was back to thinking while tired.

Gord. She couldn't remember his last name, but he'd just moved onto her suspect list. In position one.

With a plate of toast beside her at the kitchen table and tea steeping in the pot, she drew a vertical line down a sheet of paper from Anna's printer. The first column was wide enough for names, with extra room on the other side of the line for details. Later, she'd add them to her laptop file with the list of incidents.

She wrote "Gord," and across from his name, "wants inn." Although it was a long shot, "Quinn" and "spite" came next, with enough space between the entries to add notes.

Anna scooted her chair nearer. "Gord? He's not going to be prowling day and night just to own a piece of his boyhood. Plus he's bigger than the person we've seen."

"His clothes hang pretty loose. He may be smaller than we think."

"He's not well."

Landon chewed a bite of toast. The tangy jam brought a rush of saliva. "We can rule him out later. Same with Quinn. For now, we need to think through what we already know. So, who else might want the inn—or want you out of here?"

Anna lifted her palms and shook her head.

Even kind people made enemies, and Anna's caring heart might lead her places where she wasn't welcome. "You gave Meaghan and Corey jobs. Her boyfriend isn't happy... who else might be mad?"

Anna sighed. "Corey's father doesn't care. And Hart—Meaghan's boyfriend—is another stretch."

Landon added the man anyway, with "resents Meaghan working here." She included Corey, solely because of his night-time stake-out, and Nigel Foley for his unpredictable roaming. "I don't think it's them, either, but we need the full picture."

She doodled the top of the dividing line into a downward-pointing wedge. "Are there others you're helping, maybe trying to reconcile relationships or to help them change, and someone doesn't like that?"

"Since Murdoch died, I haven't had the energy. Corey and Meaghan are the only two I have on my heart right now."

Anna squeezed Landon's arm. "Which doesn't mean I've stopped loving those who don't need active support anymore."

Landon smiled. "Your love expands for each new stray."

She tapped the blunt end of her pen against her teeth. "What about someone you used to spend more time with? Maybe they're feeling neglected?"

"Not that I can think of."

Anna got up and poured them each a cup of tea. The china mugs rattled against the table as she set them down. Strain lines pinched her mouth.

Landon slid her tea nearer. "I know it's hard, but this is someone who knows you. Elva doesn't want an inn around here. Anyone else? Even a competitor? Or anyone you've argued with?"

Anna pressed her fingertips against her temples and shut her eyes. "Quinn's my only source of conflict, other than this prowler. I can't think about this anymore right now."

A tear escaped her closed lids and trembled on her lashes.

The next question died on Landon's lips. This guy had a lot to answer for.

~~~

Today Bobby had the Corvette's top down, and the salty breeze teased Landon's hair. She rescued a strand from her mouth.

It felt good to get away from the inn. She wished the wind could blow it all away—the urgency of catching the prowler, and the pressure of keeping up with her homework.

Except it was concern for Anna that had made her phone Roy's place to impose on Bobby for a ride.

She shouldn't have pushed so hard with her questions this morning. Now Anna was lying down with another headache, Timkin curled on her chest, and Landon was looking for something to cheer her up.

Inflicting her evil-twin-lookalike self on Bobby made her feel guilty, but she didn't have a driver's license to use Anna's car, and she had no one else to ask.

He slowed as they approached town. "Sure you don't want me to drop you nearer the gift shops?"

"I've been pretty inactive since I arrived. Plus, I looked up your gym online. It's close enough."

He snorted. "It's Lunenburg. Everything's close enough."

"Is that good or bad? What are you used to, anyway?" With the fancy car, Landon had pegged him as a city dweller like herself.

"Hamilton. But I like it here. Good memories of summers
~~~

with Gramp and Gran. I've been away too long."

"Roy's lucky you could come and help him for a while."

Bobby swerved around a bicyclist in the road. "My parents hired a caregiver, and he wouldn't let her in the house."

"I can't—well, okay, I can picture that. He seems like he could be... feisty."

"'Cantankerous old goat' was the expression my father used when he asked me to come. And since as a writer I don't have a 'real' job, I was the perfect solution."

The words might be bitter, but his tone was resigned.

Landon had to offer something, if only in rebellion against this man she'd never met who couldn't encourage his own son. "People read what you write. That gives you a position of influence."

Apart from the genre, she had no idea what kind of stories he wrote. Hopefully nothing too extreme, or her words would backfire. "If you can work anywhere, any time, instead of being tied to an office, that sounds like a dream job."

"Oh, it definitely has its perks. And Gramp needing me has been a blessing in disguise. My mind connects this place with good things, and I'm in no hurry to leave."

Driving, he didn't have to look at her, but he must be getting used to her presence if they could have a normal conversation. Maybe this would help him lay the past to rest.

Landon watched the buildings pass, recognizing a few. "I'd still be away, if not for Anna's trouble. The sooner those cameras arrive, the better. We need some kind of a break to catch this guy."

"You could dig a tiger pit."

"What?"

"Skip the spikes, though. Anna's too kind for that."

Landon stared. He sounded half-way serious. "Do you put things like that in your books?"

Bobby stroked the stubble on his chin like a super-villain with the stereotypical goatee. "Instead of spikes, I used a laser lattice."

"Um... did it work?"

"Nope. It was a trap for the hero. He escaped."

They reached the gym lot and Bobby parked. "I'll be about an hour and a half. Want me to meet you down by the Fisheries Museum?"

"Sure." That sounded better than coming back here to wait in the sweat-steeped facility. "I really appreciate the ride."

Landon put on the hat she'd borrowed from Anna. Ten minutes' walk brought her to the touristy part of town, with brightly-painted stores, businesses and cafés. Metal cut-outs of different types of fish hung from some of the light poles, while baskets of bright flowers decorated others.

She roamed the first gift shop, picking up teacups, pottery, and fancy marmalades and setting them down again. What could she afford that would lift Anna's spirits and not just be something to take up space?

The second shop was playing lilting Celtic music. Anna liked instrumental backgrounds for her guests' breakfasts... perhaps a new CD. Landon sidestepped woven place mats and table runners, aiming for the small display beside the counter.

A brown-haired cashier about her age was chatting with a customer as she wrapped the woman's purchase.

A chill swept Landon's scalp. The girl looked like Ciara.

It couldn't be. It was.

Their eyes met, and Landon whipped around to stare blankly at whatever the nearest table held. Behind her, the perky voice continued without a break, but she had to get out of here.

Ciara wouldn't expect her to be back in town, and Landon wore the ball cap she'd borrowed from Anna. Maybe she'd be lucky. She tugged the brim lower on her forehead and forced herself to walk calmly to the door.

The spot between her shoulder blades tingled as if anticipating an impact, even though at school Ciara's weapon of choice had always been words, not rocks.

Outside, she nearly bowled over a slight figure. "Oh, I'm so sorry!" She steadied the person's arm, then let go, preparing to duck past and escape.

Except she knew him. "Corey?"

Landon glanced back at the shop door. No sign of Ciara.

This was crazy. She and Ciara weren't the kids they'd been in grade nine. The girl wouldn't follow her onto the street to make a scene.

The logic did nothing to slow her heart rate.

Her face felt stiff, and it was hard to produce a smile for Corey. "Do you have time to talk? About Anna? As we walk?"

He peered at her through too-long bangs. "Make it fast."

She strode away from the store and turned down the first side street toward the harbour. "I saw someone Sunday night, and in the morning the car window was down. I remember her closing it. He still didn't leave any tracks, but now I know he's real."

Corey sniffed. "You didn't believe her."

"I believed she saw him, but... she's not herself. I didn't know what to think."

Nobody knew what to think. Was that what the prowler wanted? The question stopped Landon in the middle of the sidewalk. "Is that it?"

He spun to face her, eyes narrowed. "Is what it? I gotta get back to school."

School. Without thinking, she glanced at her watch. Great. Now he'd assume she was checking up on him.

The new school was farther away than the one she'd attended, but still near enough for a fast walker. Based on the time, this could be his lunch break. Or he could be skipping classes. Either way, she didn't dare alienate him.

They were on the same side in the fight for Anna. "This guy has been getting her attention when only she can see him. Sunday, he wanted it to look like Anna left the window open, so he did his best not to be seen. What if it's not about malice after all? He's trying to make her unbelievable. What if it's something else she saw, or he thinks she saw, and he wants to ruin her credibility?"

"Or he wants her to think she's losing it."

A pair of pedestrians dodged around them.

Landon started walking again. "That could be part of it, too. But this could give us a motive."

"And that'll find him how?" His final word dropped like a stone.

Typical cocky adolescent male dismissing the dumb blonde. Landon bristled, but made herself back down. She would act her own age, not his. And she needed his help. Anna needed them both.

She hiked her purse strap higher on her shoulder. "I'll ask her when I get back to the inn. Maybe if she thinks about it, she'll remember something suspicious."

"I could keep watch again." The edge to his voice said it wouldn't go well for the prowler if they met.

Landon stole a sideways glance at his slight frame and refrained from pointing out the obvious. "Anna would be devastated if anything happened to you. She installed security lights yesterday, and ordered some cameras, but he always wears a hoodie. I don't know how we'll ID him. You're there doing her yard work... have you seen any suspicious-looking people, anyone who's been upset with her lately?"

"I've been looking out for Anna since Murdoch's accident. Nobody knows who this is."

Landon caught the implication in his tone. Who was she to barge in and take over? "I'm glad Anna has people like you and Roy in her life. As soon as they catch this guy, I'm out of your hair."

"Can't wait to blow this town, can you?" He made it sound like a put-down, as if she thought she deserved better. And as if his demeanour didn't broadcast the same desperation to get away.

"I didn't mean—" Landon sighed. Defending herself wouldn't help. They reached another intersection. She paused. "Where are you headed?"

He shot her a flat stare, one side of his mouth pulling down. "Bakery on the street where we started."

Heat washed her cheeks. "I'm sorry." The shops had given way to restaurants. "I'll have to go back, too. I'm looking for a gift for Anna. This is really hard on her."

Half-way up the hill, Corey asked, "So what happened, anyway? At that store? You shot out of there looking like you were going to puke."

The careless tone said it didn't matter, but this wasn't a kid engaging in casual chat. Here was a chance to lay the first plank in a bridge between them.

"I saw someone I went to school with." Landon's spine prickled again. "You know those kids who tear down the weaker ones? It hit me all over again, and I ran."

She'd forgotten how deep the words had cut. Overreacting today meant she needed to get alone with God and let Him tend those wounds. And choose to forgive Ciara.

God had brought her this far. He wouldn't fail her now.

"Guess you're not as perfect as you seem."

The satisfaction in Corey's tone made her want to smack him. "You have no idea." But she'd been where he was. Trapped in a loser mentality, defiant and blaming everyone including herself.

Memory softened her voice. "Anna wanted to help me, even then. She never gave up. That's why I had to come back when she needed me."

Corey didn't look at her, but he nodded. His lip lost a bit of its suspicious curl. "Yeah."

Ornaments in a store window caught Landon's attention. "Sparrows."

"What?"

She pointed. "Anna always told me God cares for each

little sparrow, and He cares even more for each of us. It's in the Bible."

His shoulders twitched as if to shed the God-talk. "See you around." He walked away.

Landon's spirit sagged. So much for her clumsy attempt to plant a seed of hope in the boy, although she knew from Anna's example that it took a lot of patient sowing to make a difference.

For now, the ceramic bird would be a perfect reminder for Anna. Landon emerged from the shop carrying a small gift box in a plastic bag and hurried toward the museum parking lot.

Hoping she hadn't kept Bobby waiting, she breathed another prayer for Anna. She shared Anna's belief that God did see, did care. But she had a part to play too, if she wanted Anna's problem solved before losing her current course credit—and before someone like Ciara recognized her and started a rumour storm.

~~~

When Bobby dropped Landon off at the inn, Anna was kneeling at the flower garden. She stood, one hand pressed to the small of her back, and turned toward the car, her face shaded by the floppy brim of her hat. "How was town?"

"Quiet. I hope you didn't mind me taking off while you were lying down."

"Of course not. I don't need a sitter." The energy was back in her voice, but it still carried an un-Anna-like edge.

Landon headed for the inn. "Back in a minute."

She dropped her purse and the plastic shopping bag on her bed, and jogged back downstairs. In the kitchen, she filled two glasses with cold water and carried them outside.

"Drinks for when we need them." She set the drinks on the glass-topped wicker table, and crossed the grass to Anna. "Can I help?"

Anna peeled off her gardening gloves. "Here. Save your
~~~

nails."

Landon glanced at her fingertips. The sparkly pink polish was already starting to chip. "You're sure?"

"I can grip better without them, anyway."

Anna plucked a spindly weed and dropped it into an earth-stained orange bucket. "Is Bobby a little more comfortable with you now?"

"I think so. Apparently I look like someone he never wants to see again. It was a nasty shock for him at the airport."

Landon rubbed her nose with the back of her glove. "You don't suppose Bobby's your prowler? It sounds like this all started once he arrived."

Anna's laugh sounded almost as full as Landon remembered. "Now you're really reaching."

Yes, she was, and the worn path between the houses testified to a good relationship. She should still add him to the list with all the other far-fetched possibilities, but so far the whole list was an exercise in futility.

She brushed an ant from her leg. "I was joking about Bobby, but I saw Corey in town—"

"I don't want to hear it. You know better than to judge by hearsay."

The verbal slap froze Landon's hand above a green frond. She forced some slow breaths through her nose until the weight eased in her chest.

Concentrating on pulling the offending weed, she tried to keep the hurt from her voice. "This isn't about Corey. Talking to him gave me an idea. This guy's been messing with your head. And trying to make everyone doubt you."

"I was beginning to doubt myself. It's a terrible feeling." Anna let out a slow sigh. "I'm sorry I snapped at you. I don't know what's wrong with me lately."

"It's him. And we have to stop him." Landon could only imagine the fear of not being able to trust her own senses. She looked over at Anna. "So, what if it's not about malice?

He's trying to make you unbelievable. What if it's something you saw, or he thinks you saw, and he wants to ruin your credibility?"

Anna rolled off her knees to sit in the grass. She took off her floppy hat and used it to fan her face. "I don't remember anything raising flags. And if he only thinks I saw it, we'll never figure this out."

She stood and brushed the worst of the dirt from her clothes. "I'm ready for that drink, now."

Tugging off her gloves, Landon followed her to the deck. "You didn't report anything, or lodge a complaint or something?"

Anna plopped into a padded patio chair. She downed half of her water and set the glass back on the table. "Other than Quinn, no."

Landon sat beside her and looked out into the trees. "We could look at your planner, talk through what you did the days before this started. Where you went. Who you saw. Something might stand out."

"It doesn't hurt to try."

Anna made no move to get it, but the information could wait. They didn't need her headache coming back.

Landon sipped her drink, listening to the wind in the branches. Anna may have seen or overheard something directly, but people also confided in her.

"Whose secrets do you know? Maybe this is a preventive thing, so that if you told, the police wouldn't believe you. Like if Hart really is abusive, or if Corey named some of the kids he used to get in trouble with."

Anna tapped her fingernails against the armrest of her chair. "I've got nothing. Although a person with a guilty conscience wouldn't know his secret was still safe."

"Or maybe it's not even that. Maybe it's something he's going to do, like break into the inn, and he's discrediting his witness in advance."

"Don't let him make you paranoid." Anna took off her

clogs and carried them to the railing. Leaning over, she clapped the soles together and shook off the dirt. "I'll fetch my planner, for all the good it'll do."

"Anna, we can't give up. God gave us brains for a reason. Let's use them."

Chapter 7

Wednesday

LANDON HADN'T FELT comfortable to join Anna at her weekly prayer group. Instead, she settled in the upstairs conversation nook after breakfast to work on her paper. It was a luxury having the whole building to herself for a few hours, although an inn needed guests. The windows here overlooked the water, dark and choppy this morning.

The alcove held three cozy chairs, gathered around a round wooden coffee table. Reading lamps stood between the chairs. Landon turned one on, more for artificial sunlight than for any real need.

She stared out at the water. Yesterday, Anna's planner hadn't uncovered any memories that might point to her prowler's identity. Nor had the inn's guest book, when Landon suggested that long shot. In theory, a guest could have been scouting the area for a future crime, and Anna could have seen or overheard something incriminating. Or an angry guest could have hired someone local to exact revenge.

Realistically, with no decent leads, they were flailing in circles.

Anna had agreed to give the police Landon's suggestion

about ruined credibility as a motive, but after making the call, she'd refused to discuss the mystery for the rest of the day.

Sympathy for her friend didn't ease Landon's frustration at their helplessness, but pushing wouldn't help. Sometimes the best way to solve a problem was to think about something else and let the mind rest.

In her case, "rest" had meant finishing a short assignment for her course, and more readings for this paper she had to write.

Today her eyes were gritty. Their prowler had taken another night off, but she'd jumped out of bed each time the lights came on. She'd seen the deer again, and a few rabbits.

She felt different this morning, more settled in her spirit, as if the nightmares were easing. Maybe her idea for Bobby, about repeated exposure fading the memory-triggers, applied to her too.

Except in her case, defusing one trigger led to finding others. Seeing Ciara had freaked her out, maybe because Landon had never addressed the vague and unresolved pain from her middle school years.

In the past, Ciara's spiteful words had gashed deep. When young Landon was already vulnerable and struggling with her worth.

Ignoring her laptop on the low wooden table, Landon drew her knees up to her chest and wrapped her arms around her legs. She had to take the past to Jesus, and let Him help her forgive and let go.

Eyes closed, she hugged her legs closer to her body and rested her chin on her knees.

A buzz from her pocket jolted her half-way out of her seat. She slid back into the chair and pulled out her phone to check the alert. Her fingers and neck were stiff, as if she'd been sitting in prayer longer than she realized.

There was a new email from her professor: *This acknowledges receipt of your assignment. Kudos for submitting ahead of deadline. You do realize that class participation forms a significant portion of your final mark?*

Fingers of dread chilled her chest. Class participation was hard to achieve from three provinces away.

She buried herself in her work until Anna's car pulled into the driveway, and then stuck to it until she reached a good stopping point.

Stretching felt good. She put the laptop away and hurried downstairs, full of good intentions not to overwhelm Anna with questions until they'd had lunch.

One look at Anna's face, tight-lipped and grim-jawed, made her wish she'd come down immediately.

"What's the matter?"

"I stopped for gas on the way home. When I went in to pay, the attendant asked me if I'd be selling the inn to get away from the trouble. And a guy over by the coffee machine asked if there was really anything going on or if I was just losing it."

Anna turned to the counter and poured herself a cup of tea, her movements jerky. "We should have asked Willy to keep quiet about this."

"We need help, though. Someone might know something."

Anna splashed milk into her tea with enough force to slosh a wave over the side of the cup. With a huff, she snatched the dishcloth and sopped up the mess. "Help, yes. Not rumours tossed around in public places where tourists might hear."

They didn't need rude locals, either. Landon leaned a hip against the counter, considering the problem. As she let go of her indignation with the coffee guy, an idea formed.

"Posters. With accurate information, asking for tips."

Anna's hands splayed on the counter, fingertips white as if she wanted to dig them in. "A real prowler is as bad for business as a delusional innkeeper."

"So we put them where the tourists aren't. The grocery store, and the hardware one. Employee break room at the gas station. Corey's school, if they'll let us. Kids hear a lot."

"Whoever's out to get me would make sure word reached my guests."

"They don't need a poster to spread gossip. Come on, Anna, we need to do this."

"I'll think about it. Lunch first."

"Tea before that. Sit and collect yourself. I'll be right back."

Landon left the kitchen and trotted up to her room. The bag from yesterday lay on the bureau with her purse. She retrieved the gift box and double-checked that the clerk had removed the price sticker from under the little bird's tail.

When she returned, Anna still sat staring into her tea. Landon placed the box on the table beside her cup. "This is for you."

Anna opened the lid, and reached inside, rustling the tissue paper. She pulled out the gift, and a faint smile lit her features. "A sparrow. Thank you." She clasped Landon's hand, her eyes welling.

Landon squeezed back. "We'll get through this."

After lunch they designed a simple, letter-sized poster on Anna's computer, asking for anyone with information about the inn prowler to contact the police tips line.

Printed copies in hand, they headed for town. Landon studied the houses they passed. Could Anna's trouble be this close to home?

The houses were spread far enough apart, often with trees between them. The prowler could park along the edge of the road and sneak into the woods unseen.

She tapped the envelope of posters against her lap. "This is so frustrating. We have Gord, who wants the inn. Elva, who doesn't. Quinn, who doesn't like you. Hart, who glowers at everyone. Unless he's doing something that Meaghan might confide, there's no reason for any of them to want to discredit your word."

"Meaghan's anxious in general, but I don't think it's

because of Hart. And you've seen their car. If he's involved in something illegal, it doesn't pay well."

"It has to be someone you know, or a person connected with someone you know."

Anna sighed. "That doesn't narrow it down much. I've lived around here most of my life."

"Yes, but this only started a few weeks ago. Something triggered it."

"And I don't know what it is."

They pulled into the gas station lot. Leave it to Anna to tackle the source of her hurt first, to resolve it.

Anna turned off the car and unbuckled her seatbelt. "Coming in?"

"Strength in numbers." Landon adjusted the ball cap's brim. It wasn't much of a disguise, should they meet anyone who'd know her, but it let her pretend to be anonymous.

The attendant, a middle-aged woman with glasses, welcomed them with a smile. "Forget something, hon?"

"No, but I need some help." Anna placed a poster on the counter. "Could you put this up in your break room? The police are investigating, but extra eyes could make the difference."

"Will do. And pay no mind to that fellow who was running his mouth in here before. He's happiest when he's causing trouble."

Landon waited until they were back in the car to ask if Anna knew the man who'd been rude to her earlier.

"Luckily, no. And before you say it, he couldn't be the prowler, conveniently following me and going in for coffee while I pumped gas. Nobody arrived after I did."

"Cleverly deduced, Detective." Although it'd be nice if it were that simple. He'd be on the gas station's security cameras, and easy to identify.

They left posters at the hardware store, the library, and a few other places. At the school, the principal took one for the staff room and agreed to post another in the cafeteria.

Anna drove to the grocery store next. "This is enough for today, and we can pick up a few things while we're here."

At the customer service desk, a serious-looking teen boy with freckles assured them he'd give the poster to the employee in charge of the community bulletin board. "Good luck. I hope this helps."

Anna handed him a second poster. "Here's one for your break room, too. Thank you."

They collected a cart, and Anna produced her shopping list. It didn't take long to gather what she wanted, until they reached a cluster of shoppers in the meat department.

Anna positioned the cart in the queue. "We might find a treat for supper."

The display case held packaged steaks stickered "fifty percent off—enjoy tonight." Anna selected two. "What do you think?"

An arm shot in from her other side and snatched one of the steaks from her hands. "That one's mine."

Anna spun after it. "Hey!"

Landon placed a steadying palm on Anna's back and glared at Hart, who stood there sullen-faced and much shorter than she'd realized.

He curled a lip and waved the steak at the others in the case. "Get another one." He sauntered away with a wide-legged stride, as if he owned the store.

Meaghan darted toward Anna. "I am so sorry. That man— " She took off after him, calling his name.

The other customers in the group grumbled around them. Anna chose another steak and eased their cart out of the congestion.

Moving toward the front of the store, they heard Meaghan in the next aisle, speaking hard and fast. "What was that about? Did you even think? If you cost me this job, there'll be trouble."

Hart's reply was a grunted curse.

Anna sped up, and Landon kept pace. The more distance

between them, the better.

At least they could rule out Hart as an abusive boyfriend wanting to ensure Anna didn't report him. Meaghan was able and willing to stand up to him.

~~~

The steaks came off the barbecue tender and juicy, enhanced by Anna's tangy marinade. Foil-baked potatoes and grilled mixed vegetables completed the meal. Landon and Anna ate on the deck, savouring the food and listening to soothing Celtic music through a portable wireless speaker.

Landon slid her chair back from the table and eased her feet up on an empty seat. "Meals at home never taste this good."

"Cooking for one isn't very inspiring. I don't put as much into it when I'm alone."

Anna's hospitality, and her giving nature, meant her best efforts would always be for others.

Landon reached for her glass and finished the last swallow of water. She'd followed Anna's unspoken lead and made no reference to the prowler while they ate. They'd needed the mental break, but now it was time to focus.

"We should ask your neighbours if they have any ideas about who's bothering you, or why. And ask them to keep a lookout."

Strain lines pinched Anna's face again. "I suppose it's worth a try."

Half an hour later, they set off on foot. Anna turned left at the end of the driveway. "Roy already knows, and the woman beyond him just left on vacation."

This was the more promising direction anyway, since the broken thread had been on this side of the property.

They kept to the gravel shoulder on the narrow, two-lane road. A gust of wind off the water chilled Landon's arms. "Your neighbours won't know me, will they?"

"In a small community, you don't forget when a young
~~~

person goes missing."

Landon tracked a gull swooping low over the waves. Its plaintive cry stirred her anxiety. The hat she wore wouldn't shield her if someone recognized her name.

Thanks to her mother, none of them had ordinary names. Landon. Lacey. Leyna. Just to offset the commonplace Smith.

The sea-sharp air brought an image from early childhood, of her family at the beach. Leyna was still a chubby-legged toddler. They had loved their "special" names, then. Now, she'd bet her sisters felt like she did. Memorability made it harder to shake reputations they'd rather leave behind.

Landon's steps had slowed, and Anna looked back at her. "God can use your happy ending to help others."

"I know, but we have enough on our minds with your prowler. I don't want to add more."

They bypassed the vacant house, its "for sale" sign swaying in the breeze.

Anna led the way up the next driveway. "If there's anything to see, Elva's the sort to see it. Here's hoping."

She knocked on the screen door.

A woman shuffled toward them from the dim interior, her short-sleeved shirt hanging loose from her shoulders. Instead of opening the door, she peered at them through the screen. Her gaze locked on Landon as if checking her face against a mental list of wanted criminals.

"Something the matter, Anna?" Her voice was as suspicious as her expression.

"Yes and no. I phoned you about the prowler who broke into my car, but that wasn't his first visit. Have you seen any lights in the woods at night, or anyone passing through during the day?"

"I haven't seen anyone. And I keep a close watch."

"Well, if you do, would you phone the police? We think he comes in this way, instead of behind Roy's place."

Elva's frown narrowed her entire face. "Roy Hawke needs to keep a better eye on what's going on around him. That grandson of his, tearing up and down the road at all hours in his fancy car."

Landon resisted the urge to roll her eyes. With teens like Corey and Quinn in the area, the woman griped about an introvert who obeyed the speed limit. But he was "from away."

Elva's piercing squint stabbed her. "You're that one that was taken a few years back. Brought your mother a pile of grief. You should have known better and kept out of harm's way. Now look at yourself—ruined for life."

Landon went numb. She stared at Elva, vaguely registering the hiss of Anna's indrawn breath.

The words were nothing new, although they usually came from within. It was automatic now to put them under Jesus' authority and focus on her identity in Him.

For a stranger to throw them at her, with no warning and with so much venom... the shock stung enough that the words almost didn't register.

She swallowed, reaching for something to say.

Anna sputtered. "That is unkind and untrue. I'm sorry we disturbed you."

She turned, linked arms with Landon, and set a dignified pace along the driveway. "Don't listen to her. We should never have come."

"It's okay. What was true, I dealt with a long time ago. The rest... wow."

They reached the road, and Anna hesitated. "Should we go home? I can phone the others."

Landon tilted her head away from the inn. "You know she's watching. We don't retreat."

As they neared the next home, Landon's thoughts swirled. She'd encountered blame-the-victim mentality before, and it sprang from people's own wounds. Or from fear. But it had never carried this depth of hostility.

"That was personal to her. Even Mom's not that bitter now. Are they friends, do you think?"

"I don't know." Anna stopped and placed her hands on Landon's shoulders. "But I do know how proud I am of you. That would have crushed most people. Look how far you've come."

"I've had a lot of help. And prayer from friends like you. Now, onward. I guess, after that, we can tackle anything. Even Quinn. He's next, isn't he?"

"My friend Tricia is his grandmother. He probably won't be around."

Tricia answered their knock with a weary, guarded expression.

"It's not about Quinn, don't worry." Anna explained their quest.

The woman's face relaxed until she looked at least five years younger. "I'm sorry about your trouble. Don't think me insensitive. It's just such a relief not to have to deal with another discipline issue." She hesitated. "You're sure he's not involved?"

Anna nodded. "The police said they'd chat with the local youths, but just to find out if they've seen anything. They're not suspects."

Tricia invited them in for cookies. Blaine, her husband, was as quiet and faded-looking as she was. Their gentle welcome offered respite from the stresses of the day.

Sitting with Anna on a sagging, brown-flowered couch, Landon let the conversation flow around her. What she'd said to Anna, about being able to tackle anything now, felt true. Her reaction to Elva's vitriol proved she'd laid to rest much of the past.

She'd been afraid to come back, but Anna was right about this bringing a deeper level of healing. Too bad it took Anna's distress to force her return.

They still needed to stop this prowler, and she still had to get back to university to salvage her course, but the need to escape this place had gone.

Landon took another cookie and chewed slowly, enjoying

the awareness of peace.

When it was time to leave, Tricia beckoned her aside. "Keep an eye out for Quinn around Anna and Corey. Don't let him get away with anything, but please don't judge him harshly. It's hard for him right now."

Landon squeezed her hand. There was a story there, one Anna likely knew. God knew it too. "I'll pray for him."

Before they reached the end of the driveway, Quinn's bicycle shot in from the road. He swerved around them and doubled back to glare at Anna. "What are you complaining about this time?"

Nerves taut, Landon stepped nearer for defence, but Anna held her ground. "Hello, Quinn. There's a prowler causing trouble at the inn, and we're asking people if they've seen anyone suspicious."

His eyes narrowed. "Whatever he's up to, maybe you deserve it."

"If I do, I'd like the chance to apologize. In either case, he needs to stop trespassing." Anna looked back toward the house. "Your grandmother has fresh cookies."

The boy's sneer flickered, then returned full force. "Later." He sped up the driveway.

Landon swatted a mosquito on her arm. A tiny corner of her mind wished it was Quinn, and her conscience twinged. "You're amazing with him."

"Prayer. It's all prayer. And knowing how to bite my tongue."

They started along the road to the inn. Landon drew a deep breath of sea air. "This is personal. This guy can't be so focused on you without someone noticing."

"It's the personal part I don't understand. How can I have an enemy and not know who it is?" Anna's voice had gone high-pitched and shaky.

Landon put an arm around her. "What's your favourite dessert in town?"

"Why?"

"You've earned it, and I have a little money left to splurge with. Let's go."

It was almost dusk when they returned, taste buds satisfied by as much chocolate as they could find.

Anna rubbed her stomach. "You know it's not a good idea to combat stress with sweets."

"Of course." Landon kept her expression serious. "This was research for your guests. You need to be able to make intelligent recommendations."

"Another research tactic would be to see if there's anything worth watching on TV. In case a guest might ask."

"Lead on."

An hour or so later, Landon fetched her laptop from her room and set up at the kitchen table.

Anna stuck her head through the doorway. "Good night. Don't worry about making noise. I won't hear a thing."

"I hope those cameras come soon. Jumping whenever the lights come on is getting old fast."

"I told you, rabbits and deer. But he was ruining our sleep anyway." Anna padded into her sitting room, Timkin at her heels, and shut the door behind her.

Landon opened the file for her paper. Beside the laptop, she spread her outline and colour-coded paper notes. Speech recognition software made the writing process so much faster, and let her flesh out the details she might skip if she had to type it all. Of course, it made for some interesting phrases when the software misunderstood a word, but in the end, it was still easier.

Tired as she was, it took longer than she expected to rough out a first draft. When she finished, she queued some soft flutes, closed her work files and poured herself a glass of water. She was half asleep in the kitchen chair when the security lights snapped on.

She jerked upright, and the last of the water sloshed onto her leg. She rapped the glass down on the table and dashed to the window.

The lights showed Anna's back yard in stark relief. Nothing moved, not even a squirrel.

Something had triggered the motion sensor and ducked out of sight. An animal wouldn't do that. She turned off the inside fixture so she'd be less visible to anyone lurking in the woods, and peered outside again.

He was either hiding in the tree line or behind the barn, and she was not going out there. Instead, she unlocked the window, cracked it open, and yelled, "We've both seen you now, and the police know you broke into the car. Next time you'll be on camera. So quit the games, go home, and grow up."

Anna dashed into the kitchen. "Did you see him?"

Landon re-locked the window. "No, but the way he likes to mess with you, I doubt he ran. He heard me. The question is, will the extra security keep him from coming back?"

Chapter 8

Thursday

First thing in the morning, Anna called the police. "I'm not asking you to send anyone. He never leaves a trace, and he may not have been there. But I'd like it added to the file, please." She nodded, even though the person on the other end couldn't see her, said "thank you," and hung up.

Landon popped bread into the toaster and reached into the fridge for the haskap berry jam. "We should look anyway. He had to dive for cover pretty quickly. When's your next reservation?"

Anna blinked and paused in pouring her tea, as if she couldn't process the jump in subjects. Or couldn't remember. Then she filled the cup. "Saturday, if they don't cancel too. I don't know what to do. Meaghan needs more hours than I can give her."

The heavy tone drew Landon to Anna's side. "God's got this. And your guests won't even know there's a problem."

"Unless my unknown nemesis shows up to ruin everything." Ignoring the breakfast options, Anna slumped at the table with her tea.

Landon stepped behind her and kneaded her shoulders. This wasn't the positive, even-keeled woman she knew. They had to stop this guy before he gave Anna long-term health problems.

Anna accepted the massage briefly, then straightened. "Don't forget your toast."

Twenty minutes later, they were exploring the forest edge. The wind in the trees made a relaxing whisper, but the pine needles on the ground hid any prints.

Landon pushed a wisp of hair out of her face. The trip line she had re-strung lay broken, but so did two others farther along the perimeter. "If he came in this way, the lights might have made him take a different route to get away. An animal could have snapped the third one."

"Animals could have broken all three." Anna turned back toward the inn.

The short grass had never shown footprints before, but Landon scanned it as she moved toward the barn. He could have dropped something.

Except he hadn't.

She studied the grass behind the barn. He likely ducked in here when the lights came on, unless he'd still been close enough to the trees to beat a fast escape. In the dark, he wouldn't have had to run far to get out of sight.

If she used her imagination, she could pretend some of the grass looked flatter, as if he'd stood there. Hands on hips, she faced the wall. Anna should put a camera back here, too.

The breeze lifting the tips of Landon's hair caused movement against the wood. A dark thread, snagged in a crack at almost shoulder-height.

"Anna!"

Anna came around the side of the building. "Did you find something?"

Landon pointed. "A thread. Not much of a clue, but it's the first thing he's left." Instead of touching it, she pulled out her phone. "I'll get a picture. Then we should phone the police again."

"I'm on it."

When Anna disconnected, she said, "They'll send

someone, but it'll be a while."

Landon stared into the forest. "At least they're coming. That thread could have been there for days, but I'd still bet it's his. Nobody else would be lurking back here."

As they approached the deck steps, Nigel Foley emerged through the trees from the direction Landon thought the prowler came. He lifted his metal detector in salute. "Good morning."

Anna stopped with one foot on the bottom step. "Good morning, Nigel. How are you?"

The tall man blinked twice, then inclined his head in a half bow. "No progress yet, but I wanted to keep abreast of your happenings."

He gave Landon a similar bow.

She tuned into what Anna was telling him about the thread on the barn wall. His posture stiffened, and his head tipped to one side like a robin tracking its breakfast. Then he charged past Landon toward the barn.

Behind him, Anna called, "Don't touch anything. The police haven't been here yet."

They found him frowning at the thread. His lips moved from side to side as if he were swishing an uncertain taste of wine. He nodded, then raised one hand without moving forward to touch.

"The question is, did he simply hide here, or does something inside draw him?"

Anna sniffed. "It's just old junk."

"To you. Perhaps not to your prowler." Nigel's eyes held a definite glint. "The secrets of Captain Hiltz may not have died with him."

Landon couldn't tell from his tone if the prospect concerned or excited him. "Who?"

"The original owner of these buildings. And a sea captain of dubious repute."

Anna's smile looked tired. "Rum running was illegal, but at the time, a lot of local men saw it as a practical way to support their families. I'm sure he was no better and no worse than the others."

Nigel's face seemed to pinch. He twitched a hand at the barn. "The proof of his business ventures may lie within."

"I packed those boxes, Nigel. It's only household goods. And old furniture and equipment."

A tiny quirk of his lips suggested he held to his belief. "Should the opportunity arise, I would dearly love to investigate."

Landon focused on the thread swaying from the wall. "This is about someone tormenting Anna. If he just wanted into the barn, he could have broken in without all the theatrics."

"Motives are not always as straightforward as we might like."

Motives. Landon tipped her head to study the barn through narrowed eyes. There must be a way to find out if Nigel's words about hidden secrets came from his own mind, or if they had any basis in local lore.

Rumours like that could explain someone trying to drive Anna away from the inn. The only one who'd expressed interest to buy was Gord, but whoever this was would hardly reveal interest ahead of time.

On the other hand, if Nigel had made this up, was it innocent imaginings, or a secret desire to gain the inn property? Even his help patrolling could be part of a complicated plot to wear Anna down or discredit her.

Landon rubbed her forehead. The possibilities made her brain hurt.

The sound of an approaching vehicle drew them to the front of the barn.

Instead of a police car, a silver Lexus pulled to a stop beside Anna's car. Landon caught Anna's faint groan as Meaghan's father climbed out.

Anna stepped forward. "How was your trip?"

"It went well, thanks." He glanced at Nigel, and his

expression stiffened. "Is this a bad time?"

She linked her fingers together at her waist. "Not at all. Nigel, are you sure you don't have time for a cup of tea?"

The tall man shook his head vigorously. "I've overstayed my intentions. Please allow me to help, and… keep mum." He waggled his eyebrows. With a curt nod to Gord, he loped down the driveway.

Gord's face seemed carefully blank. "Odd duck, that one. You're sure he's not behind your trouble?"

"Nigel's heart is as expansive as his imagination. He'd never do anything to upset me."

"Unless he thought you were an alien. I've heard him talking to his cronies over coffee." Gord brushed his palms together as if dusting off pastry crumbs. "Now, as promised, I've come for your answer. May I buy the inn?"

Anna's chin came up. "I truly appreciate your kindness, but I plan to stay and face this. We have security lights now, and cameras arriving any day. Whoever this is will not end what Murdoch and I started."

"I respect that. You're a strong woman." But his eyes looked worried.

She exhaled audibly. "No argument?"

Gord's eyebrows raised. "Were you hoping I'd talk you into selling?"

"No! I just… was prepared to stand my ground."

Landon knocked one heel against the other. So much for suspecting Gord. If he were the prowler, he'd hardly give up that easily.

She needed to check out what Nigel said about Captain Hiltz's secrets. Verifying the rumour could point to other suspects. If it wasn't part of local lore, it could shoot him to the top of her list.

The first chance she had, she'd ask Roy. He'd been around long enough to hear whatever Nigel had heard, and if he didn't know, he might know who to ask.

Gord declined Anna's invitation to come in, but he leaned

a hip against his car and continued to chat. Landon was about to excuse herself and tackle her course work when she spotted a police cruiser turning into the driveway.

She hadn't expected them to be so prompt, but this would leave plenty of time to put up more posters. Hopefully Anna would check in with some of her other friends, too.

Today it was a female officer, older than Dylan, round-faced, with short brown hair. She approached Anna and held out her hand. "Mrs. Young? I'm Constable Ingerson. Is there somewhere we could talk?"

Gord pulled his keys from his pocket. "I need to be going. Take care, Anna."

Anna started around the barn as he drove away. "The thread's back here, Constable, for all the good it'll do."

Ingerson stood still. "I'll attend to that before I leave, Ma'am, but first we need to talk."

The formality, and the serious tone, made Landon catch her breath. This was how she imagined they'd deliver news of a fatality.

Anna turned, eyes wide. Wordlessly, she pointed to the deck, and then led the way.

She dropped into one of the chairs. Landon sat beside her, near enough to offer comfort if needed. Surely this wasn't bad news. Anna had borne too much already.

Constable Ingerson positioned herself across the table from them and leaned forward, brows pinched. She cleared her throat. "We had a call this morning, on our tips line."

Not bad news after all. Landon relaxed, then perked up as she caught the implication. "The posters worked."

Stern brown eyes fixed on her. "That remains to be seen. They did generate a call, which will be followed up. My issue at present is the unauthorized posting of a request for information—and civilians inserting themselves into an active investigation."

Landon's chest tightened. She glanced at Anna, then focused on Constable Ingerson. "Are we in trouble? We gave the proper tips line and website, instead of asking people to contact the inn."

Ingerson's expression didn't soften. "Our job is to protect you, which we can't do if you're involving yourselves and not keeping us informed."

Landon resisted the urge to point out that they were already involved. Instead, she tried for a conciliatory tone. "We were trying to help. This case is low-priority, and it might never be solved. But it's affecting Anna's health. Will you tell us what the caller said?"

"We received a call from a young male, saying that a man had been asking around for someone to play a joke on a friend. Apparently he was asking youths reputed to be troublemakers, and they thought he was either an undercover agent or hiding his true intent."

The officer leaned her elbows on the table, forearms crossed in front of her ribs. "If you start asking your own questions, you could compromise our investigation. We all want this solved, and I'm asking you to do your part by keeping us informed."

And by not interfering. The unspoken message came through clearly, but Landon wouldn't apologize. "What about the posters? Since they've already been seen, are we okay to put up the rest?"

"You might as well." The officer pushed back from the table and stood. "Now, if you'll point me to the evidence you phoned about, I'll have a look."

At the back of the barn, Constable Ingerson bagged the thread. "Don't get your hopes up. This could have been here for weeks, and it's unlikely we'll find a match."

After hearing their story, she made some notes and said goodbye.

Anna stood in the parking lot, arms hanging limp at her sides. Perhaps she was watching the departing car, or maybe the waves on the ocean. From her expression, whatever she saw didn't offer much hope.

Landon tipped her face toward the sun's warmth. "What a beautiful day. If I do my course work now, and you phone some of your friends from church and other places, then when we take the posters into town, maybe we could do something fun afterwards."

Anna didn't move. "She just told us not to ask questions."

"Well, we can't reveal that tip information, but we can still ask what we've been asking." She took Anna's arm and steered her toward the inn. "Or if you need a lie-down, do that instead."

The tip lingered in her thoughts. A man looking for someone to do his dirty work. That could even open it up to a disgruntled guest wanting to take revenge after he'd left. Landon pushed down the temptation to panic. Anna would know if someone had been that upset. No, this had to be someone local. Someone they could find, and stop.

~~~

Landon pushed hard at her homework, and nagged Anna into starting the calls to friends and acquaintances. She tried to follow up with Roy about Nigel's rumours, but didn't feel comfortable leaving the question as a message on his machine. She'd catch him later.

By the time they locked the inn door behind them that afternoon, they were both ready for a break. Especially since the phone calls had produced nothing but sympathy.

The prowler's actions were personal. He either had a grudge against Anna for something real or imagined, or he wanted to discredit her or her testimony, present or future. Or he was after the inn itself.

Surely among Anna's contacts, someone would have noticed something off.

As they pulled out of the driveway, Landon tapped her fingers on the posters in her lap. "Ruling out people who can't help us is part of finding the one who can. And who knows? Planting the question in their minds may cause a
~~~

clue to surface later."

Anna mumbled something, and raised her hand to a pedestrian in faded walking shorts and wide-brimmed hat. "It must be Elva's day off. I hope I didn't alienate her the other day, but love doesn't back down from the truth. She needs some positive friendships in her life, though."

Bless Anna, reaching out to everybody. This was what made it so strange for her to have an enemy. "Keep trying. She won't go to church with you, I suppose?"

Anna navigated around a pothole. "It's hard for me to get there regularly, but no. I've asked."

"Could Meaghan cover for you on Sundays, to let you go?"

Anna darted her a quick look. "I've hesitated to ask her, but she does need more hours. Want to come with me this week?"

"I was thinking of once I'm gone. But... maybe." It'd be uncomfortable, but Anna was right. The congregation would welcome her. And maybe she could get some ideas from Anna's friends, things they might not tell Anna directly.

She missed worshipping with her own church family at home. The hunger in her spirit was a good thing, and she didn't want to be away from other believers long enough to stop missing the group dynamic.

Traffic picked up the closer they came to town. They left posters at the bakery, Bobby's gym, and as many other non-touristy places as they could. Anna asked a number of restaurant and bar owners to post them in their employee break rooms, too. Wait staff always heard more than people thought.

They ran out of posters and energy around the same time, but despite all the inviting places for tourists and locals to linger, Lunenburg didn't feel restful today. Not when Landon looked at every establishment from the perspective of leaving posters.

Anna didn't protest when she suggested a change of scenery. Perhaps she felt the same.

Before long they were enjoying tea in neighbouring Mahone Bay. A few hours of roaming boutiques, and a leisurely meal in a quiet bistro, eased the strain lines on Anna's face.

A light mist started over supper, and on the way back to the inn it thickened to a drizzle.

Tomorrow would be soon enough to finish Anna's phone calls. For tonight, Landon resolved to keep things low-key and not bring up the mystery. Their prowling menace knew about the lights now, and knew there were cameras coming. That alone might be enough to deter him.

As Anna parked, Landon glanced at the barn. The padlock hung askew.

That was odd. They'd been around the barn today, but not near the doors. She went to check it out.

A ragged slash marred the shackle where it should fit into one side of the bronze body. "Anna? The lock's been cut."

She should never have told the prowler off. He came back harder, and it was her fault.

Anna ran across the deck to the inn door and rattled the handle. "Still secure here, but I don't like this. He's getting bolder."

"He must have been watching for us to leave."

Anna checked the garden shed. "This lock's fine, so the tools and mower are safe. Let me check the front door."

Landon followed her around the side of the inn. The front door was untouched. Anna unlocked it and they stepped inside.

A draft swirled around Landon's ankles. "What if he came in through one of the windows?" Her phone was in her hand before she finished the question.

Anna's face paled. "Let's find out."

Together they explored every room. Anna closed and locked the windows she'd opened in the morning. Every screen was intact, and nothing in the inn looked out of place except Timkin, who yawned at them from the middle of

Landon's bed. He glared as if they were the intruders, then jumped to the floor and trotted down the stairs.

"He knows he's not supposed to be upstairs." Anna plucked a tuft of cat hair from the duvet.

Downstairs they found him sitting by the back door. It was raining in earnest now. Anna hesitated, then let him out. "He's smart enough to look after himself." She sighed. "I'll phone this in. And then I'll make a big pot of tea to keep us awake."

Part-way through their movie, the outdoor lights flicked on. Landon jumped up and peered into the rain. Instead of their prowler, a slicker-clad officer climbed the rear steps. His hood shadowed his face. "Our officer's here."

They reached the door just as he knocked. Anna let him in. "Dylan. When we didn't see you this afternoon, I thought you finally had a day off."

"Just a schedule rotation." He stood by the door and pulled out his notebook. "Before I look around, what can you tell me?"

Anna yawned. "We went out for a few hours, and when we came home... what was it, Landon? Seven thirty?"

"Maybe ten to eight."

"Landon noticed the lock had been cut. He looped it back through the hasp, as if he didn't want us to spot it right away."

"Neither of you touched anything?"

They shook their heads.

"And no signs of attempted entry to the inn?"

"No."

"Okay, I'll see what I can find." He ducked out into the night.

They watched through the window as he roamed the yard. When he stopped at the barn door, Landon grabbed the big flashlight. "I want to see what's in there. Coming?"

"There are raincoats and an extra pair of boots in the closet. Save your shoes."

They squelched across the grass. Dylan stood in the open doorway, flashlight beam exploring the interior. "Typical nuisance vandalism, by the look of it. Or searching for something worth stealing. Be careful not to touch anything."

When they followed him inside, Anna let out a low groan. "What a mess."

Boxes lay open, their contents splayed across the wide, well-worn floorboards. A few pieces of furniture lay toppled. The hulking form of what looked like a massive dresser stood upright near the back, likely too heavy to shift.

Dylan walked the perimeter of the destruction, exploring with his flashlight. "At least he left his spray paint and matches at home."

Anna stepped farther into the barn, boots squeaking against the floorboards. "I don't even know where to start."

While Dylan investigated, Landon stayed near the door and aimed her light to probe the depths of the interior. Overhead, rafters supported a shadowed partial floor. A ladder leaned against one edge.

The building was small for a barn, and there were no stalls for animals. Perhaps the previous owners had used it as a garage for their cars. Or for storage.

The dark swallowed her flashlight beam, and the jumbled sprawl of contents made the space look smaller.

A clammy sensation crawled across the back of her neck. She focused on the destruction in front of her, and concentrated on Anna's and Dylan's voices. She had to anchor in the here-and-now. Let reality drown out the memory of her fear in the trunk of her abductor's car.

She was free. Healing. Claustrophobia was just another hurdle. She could do this.

Raindrops drumming the roof added to her sense that the walls were closing in. The air thickened. She had to get out of here.

A gust of wind banged the door shut.

She screamed and dove for it.

Momentum carried her outside. With the open door blocking most of the weather, she stood there, shoulders pressed into the wood, heaving deep breaths of damp air. Her lungs shook as badly as her hands.

Anna darted to her side. "What's wrong?"

Tears burned, and she fisted them away. "Dark space. I thought it'd be big enough. Then the door—"

Anna folded her into a hug. Their raincoats squeaked together. The pressure from Anna's arms increased, held firm, and lasted long enough to convince Landon's body she was safe.

Finally Landon could disengage. She glanced into the barn, thankful Dylan hadn't reacted to her display.

He came back to the doorway now. "I don't like the way this is escalating, but so far it's still in the nuisance category. Ladies, I'll check the loft, then I'm going to seal this and leave the details for daylight. We'll have someone here in the morning."

Back in the inn, Landon hung her dripping jacket and grabbed a hand towel from the kitchen to blot the water from her hair.

Anna picked up the kettle. "A hot drink will do us both good."

"I'll be back in a minute."

In her room, Landon changed into her pyjamas and dug out a pair of socks. Habit made her glance out the window. Nothing moved. A dim glow came from Dylan's cruiser. As she watched, the interior light went out. The car eased down the driveway.

She took the stairs slowly, reinforcing the truth to mind and body that there was no need for fight or flight.

Anna had changed too, into sleep shorts and an oversized tee shirt that said *Property of the Carpenter.* She must have read the question on Landon's face. "It's one of Murdoch's. People thought it meant the shirt was his, and then he could tell them it meant he belonged to Jesus. And why that mattered to him."

Her eyes misted. "I gave away most of his things, but I had to hold onto a few. This lets me feel like he's not so far away."

Anna's voice broke, and she turned to pour the tea.

Landon crossed the room and took the pot from Anna's hands. She set it back on the stove and faced her friend. "Hey, it's all right to miss him."

Tears stung Landon's eyes too. It was bad enough the accident robbed Anna of her soul mate. Now some low-life threatened her security.

Anna grabbed a tissue from the box on the counter and wiped her eyes. "It's like an amputation. He's been cut right out of my soul."

She picked up the teapot. "I know I'll see him again in Heaven, but times like this? That doesn't help much."

Carrying her cup, Landon followed Anna into the sitting room. She settled into a chair and studied her friend's haggard face. Anna deserved better than this. And they both needed it to end.

She set her cup on a side table and jumped up. Something had to give. Anna couldn't take much more.

Neither could she. Coming back had only proved she was still broken. She'd been crazy to think she could help Anna when she was a mess herself.

She curved her hand around the back of her neck and squeezed the corded muscles. She had to get out of here before she fell apart again.

Her heart panged. *Selfish as ever, that's me.*

She directed her pacing feet to the rain-swept window. Darkness. Not even the garden-raiding deer would leave the trees' shelter tonight.

Her reflection stared back at her, wan and distorted. Okay, so maybe she hadn't been totally selfish. She cared enough about Anna to come back. And she'd helped prove her friend wasn't seeing things. Even if all that did was make the problem worse.

Anna asked, “Is anything out there?”

“Just an old guy building an ark.”

Anna’s laugh was half-hearted. “I thought Timkin might come back while we were outside. He must have found somewhere snug to wait out the storm.”

Landon looked around the room, with its gentle lighting and homey decor. Anna had made the inn a haven, for guests and for herself. Pranks and mischief notwithstanding, Landon hadn’t been afraid until tonight.

She could blame part of that fear on her claustrophobia in the barn, but the facts said Anna’s enemy was escalating his tactics. Breaking into the car, then the barn... it didn’t take a prophet to see the inn as his next target.

The damage was increasing, too. He might trash the inn next. Worse, he might not wait for it to be empty.

She circled the furniture, feet slowing as the weight in in her spirit grew. Who was she, to think she could help Anna?

Her insistence on trying to end this had only made everything worse. She should have left it to the police. Except they couldn’t find this guy either. And as professional and able as they were, to Dylan and his colleagues Anna’s case was one of many. With more urgent calls taking priority.

Anna stood and stretched. “Want to finish our movie? Or just go to bed? Who knows what time we’ll see an officer here in the morning.”

Landon picked up her cup and took a quick sip. Lukewarm, but that was okay for spearmint. “Let’s get some sleep. I won’t be able to follow the plot now.” Not with her thoughts funnelling into self-doubt.

She lay awake a long time, trying to pray, wrestling with her helplessness and Anna’s need. If her eyes weren’t so full of hot sand, she’d look up some Bible verses to break the cycle.

A spatter of rain hit the window with a smack that made her flinch. She turned over again, but couldn’t get comfortable. Groaning, she reached for her phone.

"Do what you know you should..."

She brought up the Bible app, keyed in Psalm 23, and tapped for the audio version. The gentle words washed through her. She cued more of the verses she'd bookmarked to help with anxiety. For all the garbage online, searchable Bible tools were a major plus.

As she listened, her perspective came back into focus. So she couldn't single-handedly solve this mystery, or even protect Anna if the guy attacked. God wasn't asking her to. He was asking her to stand by Anna and share her burden.

Landon nodded in the dark. She could do that, in His strength. "God, I know You see our need. And You see this unknown enemy. Please frustrate his plans and bring him to justice. Show me how to encourage Anna, and please keep us safe."

She tapped another bookmarked verse. "And please help the police find something when they come."

Chapter 9

Friday

Despite the short night, Landon woke early. She found Anna at the kitchen table reading a devotional book. Near the door, Timkin crouched at his dish, chewing methodically.

"Look who showed up dry this morning. I wonder where he goes when he's out in a storm."

Landon snagged a banana from the wire basket and wandered to the window. The caution tape around the barn was undisturbed. "So now we wait."

"Again." Anna set aside her book and picked up her tea mug. "I have reservations for tomorrow, two couples. This needs to be settled today."

"Mm-hmm." Landon swallowed a bite of banana. She itched to get out there and hunt for clues, but messing up any evidence wouldn't help. Assuming there was evidence to find.

Dylan had said they'd see an officer in the morning, but it was afternoon before a police cruiser arrived, followed by a second one.

Landon followed Anna outside to meet them.

Constable Ingerson stepped out of the nearer car, and introduced the other officer. "Sorry for the delay. There was a bad accident toward Mahone Bay this morning. It shut down the road for a while. We've been on traffic detail."

Anna waved off the apology. "Is everyone okay?"

Ingerson's face stayed serious. "Three hospitalized locally, one airlifted to Halifax. It's pretty bad, but he has a chance."

"I hope he makes it."

"Me, too." Constable Ingerson glanced at the trees. "The file says you've been stringing thread between the trees to establish a probable vector of approach. Was that done yesterday?"

Landon nodded. "We know sometimes it's an animal, but there's usually a break in that direction." She pointed. "I didn't look this morning, since we knew you were coming."

"We'll check it." Ingerson led her colleague toward the barn. Heads together, they conferred, and then he began a ground search while she broke the tape and opened the barn doors. She fitted plastic booties over her shoes and pulled on gloves before stepping inside.

Landon went back to folding laundry, and then slogged through more of her course material.

Classroom time helped solidify what she learned on her own. Here, working alone and under stress, she could only pray she'd retain enough of what she read.

Her laptop flashed an email alert, but she made herself focus to the end of the chapter before clicking over to her inbox.

Her professor's name in the sender's field froze her fingers on the touchpad.

Opened, the message began without a greeting. *Ms. Smith. You have already missed a quiz, and obviously your class participation score is dwindling. Achieving a university degree requires setting priorities. Unless you are back in class on Monday, not even a stellar result on your paper and on the final exam will earn a place in next month's class.*

Landon stared at the words until she'd memorized them, refusing to give vent to the torrent raging inside her. Would it kill the woman to show a little compassion?

If Anna saw this email, she'd release Landon in a heartbeat and have her on the next plane back to Toronto, no matter the needs here.

She twisted her hair into a rope and tugged it. Staying meant failure, but leaving meant failure, too. Failure to stand by the one person from her past who had never given up on her.

No. She drew the laptop nearer. She could lay down her pride and obey this summons for the sake of her education, but not at the cost of leaving Anna. Not after the Lord's reassurance in the night that her role was to support her friend.

She hit "reply" to the email and paused, fingertips on the keys, searching for the best words. Finally she typed a simple *I understand, but I must stay here until this crisis is resolved. Thank you.*

Pressing "send" felt like hitting "self-destruct," but it was the right choice. She pushed up from the table and packed away her laptop.

A glance out the window showed the officers still at work. She roamed into the sitting room.

Anna glanced at her, then picked up the remote and turned off the television. "Are you okay?"

Some of Landon's stress must have shown in her face. She worked up a smile. Anna had enough to deal with. "Just lack of sleep, like you."

She plopped down into a chair. "I still wonder why this guy worked so hard to leave no trace, all those nights. Even tampering with the car was another of his mind games. And then, snip, he breaks into the barn."

She didn't mention her fear the inn would be next. If Anna hadn't connected those dots, Landon wouldn't do it for her.

There was a knock at the back door, followed by "Hello?"

Anna jumped up. "They must be finished."

Landon followed her into the hallway as Constable

Ingerson stepped inside. She heard the other officer's vehicle drive away.

Ingerson offered an encouraging smile. "This may not be as personal as we'd thought. It's a similar pattern to a string of recent break and enters."

Anna motioned them into the kitchen and clutched a chair back, as if for balance. "So it's not the same guy who's been coming at night?"

She sounded near tears, and Landon didn't blame her. They didn't have any emotional reserves left to deal with a second troublemaker.

Ingerson leaned a hip against the counter. "We can't be certain, but the night visits may have been a way of scouting the territory."

Except he could have been in and out of the barn with no one the wiser, before they installed the lights. Landon kept that observation to herself. "You said 'similar.' Were there differences?"

"There's often arson involved. As I said, this may be related, or it may not. Our intruders wore gloves, and other than a few clear footprints in the dust they didn't leave much to go on. We found vague signs of flight into the woods, but that only led us a few metres in."

"Intruders?"

"They?" Anna's squeaky question came out at the same time.

Anna had gone pale. She stood with a slight forward hunch, like she'd been hit in the stomach.

Landon pried Anna's fingers free of the chair back and guided her into the seat. She poured a glass of water and pressed it into her friend's hands. "Drink."

Anna took a few sips, then rattled the glass onto the table. "I—one was bad enough. How many?"

Constable Ingerson watched Anna, concern in the gentle furrow of her brow. "Two sets of footprints, one at the barn entrance, and one that penetrated the interior."

Colour had begun to seep back into Anna's cheeks. "I feel like they're ganging up on me. And I don't know why."

Landon rested a hand on Anna's shoulder. If she'd had any hidden doubts about her decision to stay, this erased them. Two enemies more than doubled the danger, should they plan any harm.

"Please don't worry, Mrs. Young. We *will* find them. In a small community like this, someone knows more than they're telling. Something's bound to slip."

The officer handed Anna a card. "What I need you to do now is go through the contents of the barn and make a list of anything missing. Contact us when you're done, or if anything else comes to light. Meanwhile, I'm going to canvass your neighbours to find out what they might have seen yesterday. With a special concentration on the side with those broken threads."

Anna stayed seated, but Landon followed the officer outside. She waited until they reached the driveway before speaking. "Constable, it's not just pranks anymore. What if they break into the inn next?"

Ingerson glanced back toward the inn. "If this is related to the other offences in the area, they'll move on to a new target. If it's personal, odds are it'll continue as mischief instead of danger." Her chin firmed. "But take no chances. Keep the doors locked, and call 9-1-1 at any sign of trouble."

The words were not reassuring, but at least she hadn't denied the possibility of danger. The back of Landon's neck prickled, as if someone was watching her from the trees. It was only her imagination. She refused to turn and look. "I'll feel better when our security cameras arrive."

She'd feel even better when the perpetrators were caught. Ingerson's theory about this being part of a larger pattern didn't fit. This was personal, and they still didn't know why.

The destruction seemed to up-end the idea of someone wanting to discredit Anna, but it fit someone wanting to drive her away. Or someone wanting to search the barn.

If the vandals were looking for something and hadn't found it, the inn itself could be next.

The police car drove away, and Landon went back to the inn.

She couldn't stop a glance at the forest. Nothing but trees, as she'd expected. Still, she locked the door behind her.

Anna hadn't moved, but her water glass was empty and she looked almost like herself again. She picked up Ingerson's business card and tapped its edge against the table. "How am I supposed to remember what was in those boxes?"

Landon shrugged. "We'll—" The ringing phone cut her off.

Anna crossed the kitchen and took the cordless phone from its charger. "Green Dory Inn." She pressed her palm into the countertop. "We're fine, thanks. Someone broke into the barn."

Now her fingertips were twitching. "That's really not necessary… All right."

She blew out a sigh as she put the phone back. "Roy wants to help. Just came back from an appointment and saw the police cars. Bobby's bringing him over."

"And…?"

Anna pulled a coil-bound notepad and pen from a drawer and banged it shut. "Let's get this done."

Five minutes later, Roy climbed from the passenger seat while Bobby unfolded his grandfather's walker from the back of the truck and brought it around.

Roy gripped the handles and started for the barn. "Can't wait until my leg's mended."

Bobby walked beside him. "You're down, but not out."

Landon matched her pace to theirs while Anna went ahead to open the barn doors.

The gravel path from the parking lot to the barn was short, but the walker's wheels slid in the loose rock.

Landon reached to steady Roy, but Bobby waved her off. He shook his head as if to say, "Let him do it himself."

They both stayed close enough to help if needed, but Roy reached the barn on his own and lifted the walker onto the wide-planked floor. Bobby followed him inside.

Landon stopped at the doorway. Behind the jumble of upturned boxes and furniture, bulky shapes looked like old farm equipment.

Daylight made the space easier to enter, and then Anna lit the interior. Landon looked up at the string of bulbs running the length of the building. "Why didn't you turn on the lights last night?"

"I didn't want to mess up any prints on the switch. Dylan must have thought the same." Anna squinted at the overhead setup. "The house has been re-wired, but I wouldn't want to run too much power out here, just in case."

Roy turned his walker and eased onto the seat. "Murdoch talked about getting an electrician to bring it up to code. He had a ton of ideas."

"He wanted to turn this into more guest rooms. Or a common area and games room. But then he died." Anna turned away and righted the nearest two boxes. "This one's for trash."

Bobby moved toward the ladder. "I'll look up here."

Roy scooted his seat over to another box and bent to scoop items from the floor.

Landon brought him a second box. "For rejects." She snagged a tablecloth and held it up to fold. "Anna, where did all this stuff come from?"

"The previous owner had to go into a care facility, and she sold on the stipulation that we'd keep everything until after her death. Her son disappeared years ago, and she still hopes he'll come back."

"What if he doesn't?"

"We said we'd hold an estate sale." Anna's mouth trembled. "Murdoch would never have wanted to leave me to tackle this alone."

Roy cleared his throat. "No one can take his place, Anna,

but you're not alone. Your friends will help as much as you allow."

Landon walked over to her and took her hand. "And today all we have to do is clean up. You said, yourself, you won't notice if anything's missing. Then it can sit as long as it has to."

A flurry of sneezes came from the loft. Bobby clambered down the ladder and dashed for the door. Outside, he slapped clouds of dust from his pants cuffs. He sneezed again.

"Nothing up there but spiders." Still bent over, he raked his fingers through his hair as if he felt things crawling.

When he straightened, he raised a hand in a half wave. "Hi, Nigel."

Beside Landon, Anna muttered, "Self-appointed helpers."

Landon shot her a look. "They're here because they care. We care. You'd do the same for any one of us."

"I know." Anna swiped the hair from her forehead with the back of her hand. "This would be easier if we'd had a night's sleep."

"Amen, sister."

Nigel Foley stepped into the barn and swept it with a long, open-mouthed gaze. He turned to Anna. "More trouble? Or are you looking for the captain's secrets?"

"Someone broke in here yesterday," Roy answered for her. "In broad daylight."

Nigel stiffened. He scanned the room again. "Is anything missing?"

"We don't know." Anna's words came out sharp.

His eyes narrowed. "What time was this?"

Anna shrugged. "Sometime between two and eight."

A sour look crossed his face. "With the police here yesterday morning, I intended to patrol at night. Until the rain came. Foolish of me."

Bobby tapped Nigel's arm. "Let's get that furniture off the back of the pile." He led him around the perimeter and grabbed the edge of a toppled bookcase.

While the two of them shuffled with the large pieces, Landon, Anna, and Roy worked through the smaller items.

Roy hadn't reacted to Nigel's mention of Captain Hiltz's secrets. Landon didn't dare ask him about the rumours with Nigel present to overhear. Nor did she want Anna getting defensive on Nigel's behalf.

God bless Anna's caring heart, but this trouble had to come from someone she knew. They couldn't all be innocent.

Finally Anna stood, hands pressed into her lower back. "Enough. There was nothing valuable here in the first place. Come on, everybody out."

They escaped into clean air, and Anna closed the barn door. "Thank you all. It means a lot to know I'm not alone. Who'd like a cool drink?"

Weariness filled her tone. Landon glanced at the others. "How about a five-minute hydration break, and we start searching the woods? While Anna rests."

Relief washed Anna's dust-streaked features. "Rest sounds good. But you don't have to search back there. The officers didn't find anything."

"They didn't go very deep. It's worth a try."

Nigel had a strangely closed expression on his usually watchful face. Abruptly he nodded twice, then blinked. Facing Anna, he clicked his boot heels together. "I passed this way on my bicycle yesterday, shortly before four. A car came out of the vacant drive next door."

Roy grunted. "Probably the real estate agent. But it'd be an ideal spot to park if someone wanted to sneak over here."

Nigel gave a sharp nod. "Precisely. It looked like Hart Brown's car. Unfortunately I wasn't close enough to confirm the licence plate."

Landon held back a smile. If anyone would track plate numbers, it'd be Nigel. "I don't see Hart having a motive, but it could be a clue."

Nigel's eyes narrowed. "There's trouble in that one."

"No argument here, but why would he aim it at Anna?"

Landon nudged her toward the deck. "Speaking of whom, she needs to sit. We all do."

By the time Roy had climbed the steps, Landon and Anna had filled tall glasses of water. Anna brought out a fifth chair, but Roy opted for his walker's seat. "Get too comfortable, I'll overstay my welcome."

Bobby grinned. "I'll take you home so Anna can rest, and then come back. I want to scout through to the place Nigel saw the car."

"I'll fetch my metal detector and join you." Nigel thumped his heels against the deck and made a seated bow from the neck.

Landon pictured Dorothy and her companions on the road to Oz. "The more, the merrier."

"What's going on?" Corey's voice from the stairs made Landon jump. Facing the inn, she hadn't seen him approach. When she turned, his smirk said he'd scored a point.

She pointed to the trees. "Searching for signs of whoever broke into the barn yesterday."

He muttered something too low to hear. "This is getting worse."

"And they left a big mess."

Corey faced Anna. "The forecast says rain for the next few days, so I came to mow early. I can help clean up after."

A thin smile stretched her lips. "Thank you, Corey."

He pulled a key from his pocket and jogged across the lawn to the garden shed.

The five-minute break stretched into half an hour before the men left, Bobby and Nigel promising to return. Anna went to lie down, and Landon migrated into the sitting room to one of the recliners. She leaned her head back in the chair, listening to the buzz of the mower.

When she closed her eyes, she saw the mishmash from the barn floor.

She woke with a start and sat up to work a kink from her neck. The mower still droned, so she couldn't have been out more than half an hour or so.

Bobby and Nigel must be back by now. They should have woken her. Still rubbing her neck, she went to the sitting room window.

Two figures moved, deep among the trees. No point joining them now. They'd have a system already in place.

She liked Bobby's idea of checking out the property where Nigel had seen the car, although they weren't likely to find anything helpful. It wasn't like the movies, where the villain would conveniently drop an identifying clue.

Landon crossed her arms in front of her and reached forward to stretch her upper back. Since the guys didn't need her, she might as well put some more time into cleaning up the barn mess. She found a push broom in the closet and carried it outside.

She propped the door open with the broom, and flicked the light switch. The furniture stood neatly in front of the old machinery, with the "keep" boxes nearby. A few "toss" boxes sat by the doorway. At least two-thirds of the boxes lay on top of their former contents.

Groaning, she headed for the far end of the mess. Every box she could refill now was one less to do tomorrow. Even if their vandal miraculously turned himself in today, she couldn't leave this mess to weigh on Anna's mind.

She wadded up an old quilt for under her knees and set to work. This broken crockery had to go. Too bad the former owner hadn't given it all to a thrift store in the first place. Books and knickknacks went into a box to keep, along with a handful of towels. As Anna had instructed, she didn't waste time folding.

Under a framed print of a sailing ship—for the keeper box in case Anna decided to replace the cracked glass—she found an amber-coloured, translucent serving bowl, protected by the pillow beneath it. She wrapped the bowl in another towel and nestled it carefully at the top of a box.

The next bowl she found hadn't fared as well. She dropped

the pieces into the trash box and collected a stash of gardening magazines from twenty years ago. When she picked up a hand mirror, a long shard fell out.

She pulled a dark piece of fabric from the pile and used it like a mitt to grasp the knife-edged glass. Soft and thick, it felt like sweatshirt material. The mirror shard landed in the trash with a plink, and Landon stretched out a hoodie.

Not something an old lady would likely have worn, and too new for the long-gone son.

More like what they'd seen on the prowler. Holding it up, she checked for a spot that might have snagged on the back of the barn. Her fingers found a small hole in one shoulder.

A low whistle sounded from the door. "Looks like a tornado hit."

Landon twisted around to see Corey.

His eyes locked on the hoodie. "Hey, that's mine. Where'd you get it?"

Heart racing, she stared up at him. Her voice stuck. "It... was buried in this mess."

"No way. Hey, I didn't. I swear—" His eyes were huge in a death-grey face. As if he saw disaster in the instant before impact.

Men's voices came from outside. Bobby and Nigel must have finished their search.

Corey whipped the hoodie from her hands and fled.

"Come back!" Landon surged to her feet, then slumped back onto her knees. With a head start and desperation, he would easily outrun her. And hearing the others approach, he'd have gone in the opposite direction.

A chill slid around the back of her neck. There'd been two people in the barn, which meant the unknown man from the phone tip had found a helper after all.

Corey didn't need a personal motive, if this guy had some kind of hold on him. No matter how strong the boy's loyalty, the right kind of pressure could make a person do nearly anything.

His hoodie had gotten in here somehow.

If only she'd listened to Anna and left the mess alone. She couldn't ignore what she'd found, but pointing to Corey would bring Anna more hurt.

She blinked back tears. Victim or villain, Corey was hurting, too.

Heavy-hearted, she walked out to meet the searchers.

Bobby bypassed the stairs and headed in her direction. "Nothing in the woods, and nothing but tire tracks next door. He may have been parking behind the house all along. It's been vacant since before I got here."

His gaze settled on her face. "What's wrong?"

"Corey." She held out her empty hands. "I found his hoodie inside. He grabbed it and took off."

Nigel didn't speak, but his sigh matched the wind high in the pines.

"Huh." Bobby kicked at the grass. "He definitely wasn't the guy in the back. Did you see that big bureau back there?"

She nodded.

"There were marks in the dust where he'd moved it a few feet. It took two of us to budge it. Corey wouldn't have had a chance. It doesn't make sense, though. He's pretty loyal to Anna."

She looked from one to the other, the pressure in her chest increasing by the minute. "But his hoodie was in there. This will break her heart."

She left them and plodded toward the inn. The sick feeling in her stomach wouldn't settle. This wasn't just mischief and theft. With Corey involved, it was betrayal.

Her footsteps barely made a sound on the stairs and across the deck. She eased open the back door and stepped into the kitchen. Anna had looked exhausted. If she were still sleeping...

She peeked into the sitting room. Anna lay in her recliner, eyes closed. Quiet instruments softened the air. She hadn't made it very far from bed before drifting off again.

Another half hour or so shouldn't matter. Landon slipped out her phone. She'd update the police from her room, in case Corey was a flight risk. Tell them about the car Nigel had seen.

Anna's eyelids lifted. "Landon?"

"Hey… sorry to wake you."

"I was just gathering my thoughts."

Landon crossed the room and knelt at her side. "Anna, I have to tell you something. I found some evidence in the barn."

Anna raised the chair back upright. "Finally." Her gaze sharpened. "What's the matter?"

Landon took her hand. "It was Corey's hoodie. He admitted it was his. He denied everything else, but then he ran away."

Anna's grip tightened. Her lips flattened, as if clamping down on the pain.

"I'm so sorry."

Anna's eyes took on a hard glint. "And you're sure he's guilty no matter what he said."

Landon ignored the challenge in her tone. "You didn't see his face." She rubbed her thumb against the back of Anna's hand. "Remember, there were two people. The other one could have forced him into it somehow. We can't deny the evidence."

She held Anna's gaze. "I'm not judging him. Life is hard."

"Circumstantial evidence isn't proof."

"I know, but unless he caught the guy in the act and isn't telling what he knows, somehow he's involved."

"Or someone wants us to think so." Anna's voice held an edge.

Landon gave a sad smile. "Break and enter, minimal damage… Even the earlier things were only mischief, for all the stress they caused. Quinn might set Corey up, hoping to get him into juvenile detention, but how would he get Corey's hoodie? And it wouldn't make sense for anyone else to do it."

After a minute, Anna breathed out the ghost of a sigh. "I know that boy. He couldn't have deceived me all this time."

Landon let go of her hand. "We have to report this."

Anna seemed to age visibly. She sank back in her chair. "Would you do it? I need to pray."

After phoning in the information, Landon wandered back to the barn and picked through more of the mess. She had no mental focus for her school work, especially since refusing her professor's ultimatum effectively guaranteed a failing grade.

Part of her wished Bobby and Nigel had stuck around, but maybe it was better to be alone. Progress would be a lot slower, but she could process what had happened.

Anna probably had her Bible out, speaking God's word back to Him in prayer for Corey, for truth, and justice, but Landon's thoughts were too jumpy for anything that straightforward. Out here, in the mindless movement, she could breathe fragmented prayers for Anna, Corey, and herself. Even for the police, trying to solve this, and harder, cases.

When hunger pangs sent her inside, there was still no sign of Anna. Landon washed up, and prepared a simple supper. She set the table with extra care, and turned on some instrumental worship music.

Anna barely ate, and spoke even less. Landon told her about Bobby and Nigel's fruitless search, and then let the gentle music do its work.

Finally Anna gave a sharp sigh and pressed her palms into the edge of the table. "Enough's enough. God has to deal with this, because it's beyond me. I'm sorry I've been such a miserable companion, especially when you made this lovely meal."

Landon reached across the table and touched her hand. "I wish none of this had happened, and I hope Corey's okay, but I'm not sorry I had to come back. Maybe a person can come home again, as long as she knows it won't be the same."

In her case, that was a good thing.

By the time they'd cleared away the dishes, the rain had started. Tonight Timkin stayed in, and he followed them into the sitting room and leaped onto Anna's lap. They were trying to distract themselves with a travel documentary when a knock came on the back door.

Landon rose. "I'll get it."

Dylan stood on the deck, rain dripping from his yellow slicker. "Shelter for a soggy wayfarer?" His face was as serious as always, but there was a new glint in his deep brown eyes.

"Come in." Landon ducked out of his way. "Anna, it's Dylan."

When Anna joined them in the hallway, Dylan asked, "There's been no contact with Corey?"

"None." The word came out flat.

His lips twitched. "If he does communicate with you, I need you to give him a message. Corey is not a suspect, but we would definitely like to talk with him. Will you pass that on?"

Her whole face brightened, and her hands lifted as if she'd have hugged him if he weren't so wet. "Not a suspect?"

Dylan's gaze swept them both. "We have an individual in custody who has admitted to using Corey's hoodie in an attempt to cause trouble and deflect blame from himself."

The pressure in Landon's chest broke like an invisible band. Her lungs pulled a huge breath of air. "Who? And why?"

Dylan shifted his feet into a wider stance. "I'm sorry, I can't tell you that. It'll all come out in due course."

Anna narrowed her eyes, as if she was having trouble seeing how the pieces fit together. "How did you find him?"

"He was seen travelling through the woods away from the scene at about the same time Nigel Foley saw the suspicious vehicle."

Nigel had been on the road. He couldn't have seen anyone among the trees well enough to identify him. One of the homeowners must have spotted the culprit. And this couldn't be the guy who drove away, because there were no other houses between here and where he'd parked.

Why hadn't they left together? Maybe the car was unrelated after all—a drug deal or something. Or maybe the person in custody lived nearby. Like Quinn.

Dylan gave his head a quick shake, as if he'd followed her train of thought and wanted it to stay unspoken. "I've said this much for your peace of mind, but please keep it to yourselves for now. Our suspect has provided information that should lead to a second arrest, and we don't want to alert our target."

Landon took Anna's hand. "I'm glad you were right about Corey."

Anna squeezed back for a long moment before pulling free. "Dylan, thank you so much, to you and your team. Do you think this is really the end of it?"

His lean cheeks softened in a smile. "It looks that way. We haven't caught up with our second suspect yet, but we don't anticipate trouble. For tonight, keep your doors locked and call 9-1-1 if you have any cause for alarm. One of us will be in touch tomorrow."

They watched him dash through the rain to his car, and then Anna took out her phone. "Corey hasn't been answering my texts, but I'll send him what Dylan said."

How did Quinn, or whoever it was, get Corey's hoodie in the first place? Unless—when Corey was here mowing, last week, Anna had picked it up and left it on the deck railing. Landon had assumed Corey took it home, but the way their prowler had skulked around, he could have lifted it first.

Landon waited for Anna to finish her text. As they walked back to the sitting room, she said, "I'd love to know who saw him leaving the scene through the woods."

Anna dropped into her chair but she didn't pick up the remote and re-start their show. "I'll phone Elva. If Roy had seen someone, he'd have told us. It couldn't have been too much further afield, or they wouldn't have connected the person they saw with the inn. It's not like he would have been carrying a bag of loot."

After a brief conversation, she set the phone on the side table. "The police told her not to mention his name. So she described him instead." She blew out a deep sigh. "Quinn. My heart goes out to Tricia, but I can't call her because I'm not supposed to know."

Quinn could definitely have sneaked back to take Corey's hoodie from the deck railing. Planting it in the barn to implicate his former friend made sense.

As a prowler, the boy's attitude was a definite fit, but not his method. "He must have been the helper. Following instructions, and not doing this on his own. That's why it didn't seem like what he'd do."

Maybe the guy had pressured him, like she'd thought could have happened to Corey. But with Quinn's hostility to both Anna and Corey, he wouldn't have needed much pressure. Just a firm hand to make him stick to the plan.

Landon leaned her head against the upholstery. As sorry as she was about Quinn, an end to this felt surreal.

If they caught this second guy as soon as Dylan seemed to expect, she could be back in class on Monday after all.

She held back a sigh. Too bad she'd been so quick to refuse her professor's ultimatum. Still, if she showed up on time, the woman couldn't complain.

Anna yawned. "When this is finally over, I may sleep for a week. Tonight I'm concerned about Corey, Quinn and his family, and..."

"And what?"

"If Quinn was the helper, who was he helping? Who among my acquaintances would have done this, and why?" Her palms flattened on the chair's armrests, fingers stretching wide. "I'm not sure I want to know."

"But you want it finished. Think how good that will feel, instead."

Chapter 10

Saturday

Morning came with no word from Corey, or from Quinn's family. Tricia must know Anna wasn't the kind of friend to turn against her, but still, reaching out would be hard. Landon hoped they soon got the official word from the police so Anna could comfort her friend.

Anna stood at the kitchen counter making fresh cookies to welcome the day's guests. "I have an inn to run, and my thoughts will have to sort themselves out in the background. I can pray while I work." Rounded shoulders and wide-planted feet spoke of the burden she bore.

The grey day didn't help. Landon pulled out a chair and sat watching her friend. She reached for the little sparrow ornament on the table, and spun it aimlessly with her fingertips.

A heavy motor sounded outside. Anna looked out the window. "Delivery. Could you get that? My hands are covered in cookie dough."

Landon signed for the package and carried it back to the table. "The cameras are here, for all the good it'll do now. If we'd had them on Thursday, the barn might not have been broken into. Or we'd have had an alert, and called the police in time to catch the vandals."

Anna turned from the trays of cookie dough, her eyes brimming. "And Corey wouldn't have run away. A young boy like that, anything could happen to him."

"I know." Landon closed her thoughts to worst-case fears and committed him again to God's care. "Maybe he thinks his phone can be used to track him. That would explain him not seeing your texts."

This time of year, sleeping somewhere in the woods wouldn't hurt him when it was dry, but last night in the rain would have been miserable. And he'd be hungry. He'd be afraid to come here, and probably the only ones he could trust to hide him were his former friends, who'd only lead him back into trouble.

He already thought he was in trouble, so what would hold him back? *God, You see Corey... keep him...*

Meaghan stuck her head in the back door. "Sorry I'm late. I had to get Dad to drive me. I should still have everything done before check-in time."

Gord followed her inside. "You two look wiped out. What happened this time?"

Landon's hands curled into fists on the tabletop. "The barn was ransacked on Thursday. We spent yesterday on cleanup."

Meaghan glanced toward her father, then she turned away. After she hung her coat on a peg in the hallway, she set her bag against the wall and pulled a basket of cleaning supplies from the cupboard. "I should get started."

Anna stepped toward her. "What's wrong? If you're not feeling well, Landon and I can get the rooms ready."

Gord pulled his daughter into a one-armed hug that triggered a muffled sob. His brows came together. "I think Meaghan and I have the same concerns."

The young woman flinched, but said nothing.

Keeping his arm around Meaghan, Gord scowled. "She asked me to drive her because the police are talking to her boyfriend. They requested she not use the car until they'd searched it. And they asked her about his movements on Thursday. Perhaps now we know why."

So Nigel had been right about seeing Hart's car.

Landon picked up the little sparrow again, pressing her fingers into the sculpted feathers. She couldn't look at Meaghan. Including Hart in her list of possible suspects hadn't prepared her to consider the effect on his family.

She'd never really believed it could be him. Lots of people were rude. It didn't make them criminals.

As much as she wanted to see this solved, Hart as the culprit didn't make sense. Unless there really was a local rumour about the sea captain's mysterious secret. Then it wouldn't be personal after all. Anna had simply been in the way.

Something like a growl rumbled in Gord's throat. "Anna, I have never had a high opinion of my daughter's boyfriend, but I never suspected he was the one causing you all this trouble."

Meaghan slid from his hold and stood staring at the floor, twisting her hands together. "Do you want me to go?"

"Of course not." Anna held out a hand. "Even if Hart turns out to have done this, you can't be blamed for his actions. If you need to go today, by all means do, but please come back."

Gord beamed at Anna before turning to his daughter. "If I take you home now, you'll just stew over it."

Meaghan choked out a muffled response, grabbed her cleaning basket, and fled from the room.

Landon started after her, then settled back into her chair. Whatever the other girl was feeling, she clearly needed some time alone before she'd be ready to talk.

Anna slid the cookies into the oven and set the timer, then turned to Gord. "I'll drive her home when she's done."

After a gentle heart-to-heart? Landon could cover check-ins if the guests arrived. Let Anna do what she did best with hurting souls.

Gord walked to the window and looked out. "I'd

wondered about that oddball, Foley, and here it was much closer to home. While I'm here, let me help with the barn cleanup. Unless you've finished already?"

"Thank you, but no. You're a good friend—with a heart condition. If Hart made the mess, he can clean it up. If not, when they find Corey, I'll pay him to do it."

Gord looked back at Anna. "Find who?"

"The boy who does my lawn. Someone planted his hoodie in the barn. He's run away."

"Maybe they were working together." His narrowed eyes glittered. "A no-account man and a kid. The blind leading the blind."

The lines deepened around Anna's mouth. "Two sets of footprints were found in the barn, but the police say Corey's not a suspect."

"So there's still someone out there."

Landon tapped her fingertips on the table. It shouldn't hurt to tell him the other suspect was already in custody, without mentioning Quinn by name, but she'd obey Dylan's instructions to keep it quiet. For all they knew, Hart was only another source of information and not the guilty party.

Anna didn't say anything, either.

"I can't think who he'd talk into taking the fall with him." Gord rested his hands against the counter behind him and leaned back. "The cops seemed pretty sure they had their man."

Anna sat beside Landon at the table, and gestured to Gord to join them. He shook his head.

"Wait a minute..." Landon looked from Gord to Anna. "One of the intruders moved a heavy bureau in the back of the barn, all by himself. Hart's not big enough." Nor was Quinn.

Gord's face darkened. "He's scrawny, but he's a scrapper. Spends a lot of time pumping iron instead of working his so-called second job."

Anna crossed her forearms on the table and leaned into

them. "What on earth does Hart have against me? We've barely spoken."

Gord tipped his head back and studied the ceiling. "It's not you, it's my daughter. He wants her at home, cooking and cleaning for him, not out working for someone else."

"Could they live on what he makes?" Anna's question echoed Landon's thoughts.

Gord huffed. "That makes him even more resentful. He wants to be sole provider and boss, but he's a follower in a dead-end job. He resented Meaghan working here from the beginning, but I thought he'd smartened up. She was in a gift shop in town before this. He cost her the job by hanging around and mouthing off at the owner."

Landon studied Anna's profile. "So it wasn't someone with a personal grudge against you. That's a relief."

"It would be, if I didn't feel so bad for Meaghan. At least it's over, and I can breathe again."

Gord tapped his palm against his fist a few times in rapid succession. "You've been so good to Meaghan, and Hart tries to ruin it all."

His mouth formed a grim line. "He was supposed to be at the plant on Thursday, but it wouldn't be the first time he's skipped work to do his own thing. I don't know how she puts up with him."

The timer beeped, and Anna cracked open the oven door for a peek. She closed it and reset the timer. "You picked a good morning to come, Gord. We'll have fresh chocolate chip cookies in a few more minutes."

He ran a hand over his stomach. "I wish. My cholesterol's still too high. But I'll take you up on the offer to drive Meaghan home. That'll let me go see what's up with her no-account boyfriend. I shouldn't say this, but I hope they lock him up. Maybe he'll learn something."

"I'll take her home." Anna peeked into the oven again, then turned off the timer and slid her hands into her oven mitts.

Once the steaming trays rested on pot holders on the counter, Gord left.

When the door closed behind him, Anna slid open a drawer and pulled out a cookie lifter. "If you'll put the cookies on the cooling racks, I'll phone and see if the police can confirm anything."

Landon eased the chocolate-studded, golden cookies from the trays and positioned them on the racks. Her professor's ultimatum vibrated in her thoughts. Anna mattered more than the teacher's demands, but an arrest now would free Landon to go home in time to salvage her grade.

She'd nearly finished with the cookies when Anna walked back into the room and set the phone on its base.

Anna's smile told the tale, and already her face looked less pinched. "They didn't want to tell me anything, but when I threatened to show up in person they did confirm that charges will be laid against two people for the break-in. No names were mentioned, but from what Gord said, this second one has to be Hart. Poor Meaghan. And here I thought it was all about me."

Charges would be laid. It was official. Weight slipped from Landon's shoulders.

Anna's troubles were over. No more prowlers, no more fear for her business.

Landon wanted to dance. Instead she picked up a cookie. "I'm sorry for Meaghan, and for Quinn's grandparents, but for us it's time to celebrate."

The cookie was crispy on the edges, gooey in the middle, just the way she liked them.

So much for her ideas about the motive behind it all, but Gord's assessment of Hart's character explained a lot.

Even the random leap from mind games to destruction made sense as a resentful man's response to Landon's challenge, the night she shouted at him to go home and grow up.

What had he hoped to gain? Forcing Anna to give up the

inn so Meaghan would lose her job? How many jobs would he cost her before she quit trying to work? Or before she quit the relationship?

Landon popped the rest of the cookie into her mouth and licked a chocolate smear from her fingertips. She didn't have to understand Hart. The police wouldn't have arrested him without reasonable cause. If they were satisfied, she would be too.

The main thing was that the trouble had ended. Anna could focus on her inn, and continue her husband's legacy with Corey—once the boy was found.

Landon could go back home knowing Anna would be okay.

The thought of leaving brought an unexpected pang of regret, not just for Anna, but for this place that once was home. She'd missed the ocean.

"Anna... with this solved, I need to be in class on Monday. If Roy can re-book my flight, would you drive me to the airport?"

Some of the sparkle left Anna's eyes. She nodded slowly. "I hate to let you go, but it's put your course at risk being here this long."

If she only knew. Landon prayed there'd be enough time to appease the professor before the exam.

She couldn't dwell on that now. Instead, she smiled at Anna. "You were right. Being here brought healing I didn't know I needed."

Anna drew a shuddering breath. "Speaking of answers to prayer... pray with me? For Corey to be found safe? And for Tricia and Meaghan?"

Tears pricked Landon's eyes. "We will fight for them. Together, even when I'm back home."

AUTHOR'S NOTE

Well, **what did you think** of my imaginary friends at the Green Dory Inn? Keep turning pages for some discussion questions and a hint of what's to come in the next book.

Human trafficking is all too real a problem, both for sex and for labour. It's possible for survivors to heal as well as Landon is healing, but I didn't find very many positive reports. The truth is ugly and frightening, and sex trafficking victims can be girls and boys as young as 12. Or younger. One way to fight back is to support your local programs for at-risk youth.

A few sites for background information:

- Canadian Centre to End Human Trafficking canadiancentretoendhumantrafficking.ca
- Public Safety Canada canada.ca/en/public-safety-canada/campaigns/human-trafficking.html
- Canadian author K. L. Ditmars lists more resources on her website: klditmarswriter.com/resources

If you are or someone you know is a victim of human trafficking, please reach out for help!

- In Canada: Canadian Human Trafficking Hotline canadianhumantraffickinghotline.ca
- In the US: National Human Trafficking Hotline humantraffickinghotline.org/get-help
- In any country: in your internet browser, type "human trafficking help" and add your country.

To end on **a brighter note**: In case you're concerned about **Corey**... he will reappear fairly quickly in the next book, *Hidden Secrets.* For now, he's found a perfect hiding place.

For **advance notice** of future releases, be sure to subscribe to my mailing list at bit.ly/JanetSketchleyNews or follow me on Bookbub at bit.ly/JanetSketchleyBookBub.

Finally, a favour if you're so inclined: Could you drop a **brief review** on Goodreads or your favourite online bookstore? Nothing fancy, just mention what you liked or didn't like, and why. No spoilers, please!

Thanks for spending time at the Green Dory Inn, and I hope you'll come back again! For a sneak peek at **what's next** in the Green Dory Inn series, keep reading. The next book, *Hidden Secrets*, is **a full-length novel**.

Acknowledgements

A huge thank you to editor Marcy Kennedy, and to the following people who provided further editorial input, brainstorming help, and proofreading: Matthew Sketchley, Russell Sketchley, Heidi Newell, Janice Dick, Ginny Jaques, Ruth Ann Adams, and Beverlee Wamboldt.

A special shout-out to my newsletter subscribers who so cheerfully pitched unusual ideas for how Roy injured his leg. He'll tell everyone what happened in the next book.

Thank you to Emilie Hendryx for creating a cover I'm proud to display.

Special thanks to my family for their support, and above all, to Jesus. Words aren't enough.

Discussion Questions

1. How important is place to you in a story? Do you prefer to read fiction based in settings you know or those unfamiliar to you?

2. Nobody dies in this story. How do you feel about a murderless mystery?

3. As children, Landon and her sisters, Leyna and Lacey, loved their uncommon names. Is there something noticeably distinctive about you? Do you like it or try to downplay it?

4. Anna's encouragement has played a large part in helping Landon find her way to faith and begin maturing in that faith. Do you have an Anna in your life? Are you an Anna to someone else?

5. Landon must choose between succeeding at school and supporting her friend. She frames the decision in the negative: failing her course or failing her friend. Is it easier for you to break down a hard choice by contrasting what could be gained or what it could cost?

6. People often say, "You can't go home again." In what ways is that true? In what ways is it not?

7. Landon sees her restoration from her traumatic past as "I am healed. I'm being healed. I will be healed." In what ways do you see progressions like this in your life or in those around you?

8. Landon thinks if Bobby can get used to her presence it might help him lay his past hurts to rest. And she hopes time spent in her hometown will make it easier to be back. In what ways does repeated exposure to a negative stimulus reduce its effect? How might this be a good thing? How not?

9. Misfits and the wounded seem drawn to Anna. She can't fix their problems but she shows them love and dignity. Do you recall a time when someone showed extra kindness to you?

10. In her distress, Anna the helper walls herself off from the help of her friends. How does a person reach out to a friend who's raising barriers? When is it wise to respect their distance, and when do we need to persist?

11. Elva's tirade at Landon reveals more of her own hurt than she knows. If we could stop and think when someone spews vitriol at us, what might we discern about their needs? How might it change our response? How might we create a pause to allow this instead of retaliating?

12. After the barn break-in, Landon is upset and knows she should turn to Scripture and worship but doesn't immediately do it. How often do we try to tough it out on our own instead of turning to the sources of help we know and trust? What are some positive coping mechanisms that can be part of our regular mental self-defence?

Next in the Green Dory Inn Mystery Series:

Hidden Secrets

The secrets of Captain Hiltz may not have died with him.

When Landon Smith returns to the Green Dory Inn, she finds innkeeper Anna Young still shaken by the recent vandalism and unable to cope when the inn is targeted in an online vendetta. Prickly neighbour Bobby Hawke can help with Anna's cyber woes, but when the attacks escalate to physical threats Landon and Bobby must work together to unmask the culprit.

A cryptic message about a tunnel points to the original owner, a notorious Prohibition-era sea captain rumoured to have left hidden wealth. Contraband, treasure, evidence of things better left buried...

How far will Anna's enemy go to claim the tunnel and its contents? Protecting Anna will require courage and faith as Landon battles the locals' attitudes and the scars of her past. Even then, she and Bobby are tracing the faintest of clues. With Anna on the brink of emotional collapse—and danger rising like the tide—time is running out.

~~~

Order your copy now in print or ebook from your favourite retailer, or request it from your local library.
~~~

YOU MIGHT ALSO LIKE JANET SKETCHLEY'S REDEMPTION'S EDGE SERIES:

Heaven's Prey (book 1)

A grieving woman is abducted by a serial killer—and it may be the answer to her prayers.

Despite her husband's objections, 40-something Ruth Warner finds healing through prayer for Harry Silver, the former race car driver who brutally raped and murdered her niece. When a kidnapping-gone-wrong pegs her as his next victim, Harry claims that by destroying the one person who'd pray for him, he proves God can't—or won't—look after His own. Can Ruth's faith sustain her to the end—whatever the cost?

Secrets and Lies (book 2)

A single mother with a teenage son becomes a pawn in a drug lord's vengeance against her convict brother.

Carol Daniels thinks she out-ran her enemies, until a detective arrives at her door with a warning. Minor incidents take on a sinister meaning. An anonymous phone call warns her not to hide again.

Now she must cooperate with a drug lord while the police work to trap him. Carol has always handled crisis alone, but this one might break her. Late-night deejay Joey Hill offers friendship and moral support. Can she trust him? One thing's certain. She can't risk prayer.

Without Proof (book 3)

"Asking questions could cost your life."

Two years after the plane crash that killed her fiancé, Amy Silver has fallen for his best friend, artist Michael Stratton. When a local reporter claims the small aircraft may have been sabotaged, it reopens Amy's grief.

Anonymous warnings and threats are Amy's only proof that the tragedy was deliberate, and she has nowhere to turn. The authorities don't believe her, God is not an option, and Michael's protection is starting to feel like a cage. How will Amy find the truth?

Janet Sketchley is an Atlantic Canadian writer who likes her fiction with a splash of mystery or adventure and a dash of Christianity. Why leave faith out of our stories if it's part of our lives?

Janet's other books include the Redemption's Edge Christian suspense series and the devotional books, *A Year of Tenacity* and *Tenacity at Christmas.* She has also produced a fill-in reader's journal, *Reads to Remember: A book lover's journal to track your next 100 reads* (available in print only, with two different cover design options). You can find her online at janetsketchley.ca.

Subscribe to Janet's newsletter at bit.ly/JanetSketchleyNews, or follow her on BookBub at bit.ly/JanetSketchleyBookBub.

Manufactured by Amazon.ca
Bolton, ON